CODE NAME:

CLONE

CODE NAME: CLONE

BY MARGARET C. COOPER

Illustrations by Christopher Bigelow

WALKER AND COMPANY NEW YORK, NEW YORK

First published in the United States of America in 1982 by the Walker Publishing Company, Inc.

Published simultaneously in Canada by John Wiley & Sons Canada, Limited, Rexdale, Ontario.

ISBN: 0-8027-6474-6 Trade
        0-8027-6475-4 Reinf.

Library of Congress Catalog Card Number: 82–60101

Book design by Robert Barto

Printed in the United States of America

10 9 8 7 6 5 4 3 2 1

For Connie, Frances, Vivian

1

STEFAN lay rigid inside the mammoth jet liner as it lifted off the ground and sped smoothly upward. He fumbled with the fastenings of his thermal sack, snapped open the lid of the stout crate he lay in, and sat up.

Next to him, the lid of a similar crate opened and his brother's tousled head appeared. "Airborne at last!" Evonn shouted above the ascending throb of nuclear-powered engines. "Do you think we'll really make it through American customs in these crazy boxes?"

Stefan shrugged. "Well, I was afraid we'd never be able to escape from Stovlatz, but we did. Then I was afraid Professor Lev's friends wouldn't be able to smuggle us out of Vienna, but they did. So maybe we'll get into the country safely, too, and finally begin the search for our father."

Evonn struggled out of his thermal sack and climbed out of the crate. "What a huge baggage compartment!" he said.

Stefan climbed out, too. They began to examine the boxes and crates that surrounded them.

"Hey, I found a cat." Evonn bent close to the small cage. "The tag says: 'Nefertiti, gray Kaffir'—that's an ancient Egyptian breed, you know. Sleep on, little Egyptian cat; somewhere your 'mummy' is waiting for you." He giggled at his own joke.

Stefan was too absorbed by his own discoveries to notice. "These big cartons must be artifacts—they're going to an American museum," he called. "Oh, Evonn, look at this German shepherd! A farmer I knew had one just like him. I feel sorry for him, squeezed into that little cage."

Evonn joined Stefan and they knelt in front of the sleeping dog.

"All these animals must be tranquilized," said Evonn. "Five solid hours locked in a cage would really knot their neurons!"

"Maybe we should have taken our sleeping pills, too," said Stefan. "I'm going to take one before we land. I was really nervous inside that crate while they were loading us aboard."

"Now I can see why it took so darn long!" Evonn exclaimed. "All these boxes are labeled for special care. Let's see what ours say." Evonn tilted his crate up to the light from one of the narrow slit windows. "There are 'Fragile' and 'This side up' labels pasted all over it. The tag says: 'Matched Statuary, (two), "CUPID WITH BOW", Property of Janos Keplosz'."

"Good old Janos," said Stefan. "I'm glad he and Peter Rubjak are going to get us right at the airport." He wrestled his crate into an upright position and read the tag. "Mine says the same thing. 'CUPID WITH BOW'—I wonder who thought that up. But it is true that we're a matched pair, isn't it?"

"Well, we're clones, and that's about as matched a pair as you can get." Evonn studied his brother's face. "You know, I still haven't gotten used to it. For thirteen-and-a-half years I thought I was an orphan with no relatives; then suddenly I find out that I have a brother—a clone-brother at that. What a shocker!"

Stefan nodded. "I still hate the idea that Dr. Zorak cloned us. It makes me feel like something that crawled out of a test tube." He pulled the thermal sack out of his crate and wrapped himself in it before he sat down. "But as soon as I found you, I knew I'd never have that awful lonely feeling again."

"Hey, Stefan, what do you think is happening back at the Scientific Research Station at Stovlatz?" asked Evonn. "I hope Zorak got into big trouble when they found out we escaped right through their laser barriers."

"When *who* finds out? No one finds out anything about Stovlatz unless Zorak wants them to."

"But what about those government officials who were touring the station?" protested Evonn. "Won't they suspect that something strange went on the night we escaped?"

"They're only interested in Zorak's nuclear research and weapons-design work. As long as that goes according to schedule, I doubt if they care about his personal experiments."

Evonn sank down beside Stefan. "Well, Zorak won't give us up easily. He's been scheming for too many years to use us for his own purposes."

A series of dull thuds interrupted the boys, and something moved across the floor.

Stefan clutched Evonn's arm. Both boys froze.

"Somebody's in here!" Stefan hissed. He made a dive for his crate.

"Relax, Stefan. It's that dog. He must be waking up or having a nightmare."

They crept across the floor and looked down into the dilated pupils of the huge shepherd. The dog struggled to stand up, and, as he did, the cage tilted and slid forward.

"Lie down, boy. It's all right," said Stefan in a soothing voice. "Poor fellow. You'd think by this century there would be a better way to transport animals."

"Oh, the cage is okay; it's just too small. Or he's too big."

At the sound of the boys' voices, the dog perked up his sable-tipped ears and whined.

Evonn kneeled down and flipped over the cage tag. The sudden movement startled the animal and a powerful, rumbling growl sounded deep within his throat.

"Well, that figures," said Evonn, dropping the tag instantly. "His name is 'Donner'—that's 'Thunder' in German.

If he sounds like that when he's half-asleep, imagine what he's like when he's alert."

"Where's he being sent?" Stefan leaned forward gingerly to read the address label. "This is strange, it says his owner is P. Rubjak! I didn't know Peter had a dog, did you?"

Evonn shrugged. "No, but he joined us only a week before we left Vienna, and Peter Sour-puss hardly spoke two words to me."

Donner seemed to follow their conversation with interest from the first mention of his name. Now he whined and began to scratch furiously at his molded plastic cage.

"He'll injure himself if he keeps that up!" exclaimed Stefan.

"What can we do? We can't let him out; he might bite."

Stefan shook his head. "Shepherds aren't likely to make an unprovoked attack. He knows we're friendly."

An eager bark from inside the cage seemed to indicate agreement.

"That settles it!" Stefan declared. "He's coming out!"

The cage was bound with a thick strap, which the boys unfastened with difficulty. Both sides fell open at once, like an upright suitcase.

"We should sit quietly and let him get used to us," Stefan murmured, sinking to the floor.

Donner leaped gracefully out of the cage bottom and stretched his powerful rear legs. He approached the boys, sniffing each one thoroughly, and after an indifferent inspection of the sleeping cat, returned to Stefan and Evonn. With a contented sigh, he settled himself between them.

Evonn stared delightedly over the massive head at his brother. "He likes us."

They stroked the warm, furry body with increasing confidence, and Stefan fed him a protein bar he found in his pocket.

"Wouldn't you love to have this guy along with us if Zorak showed his ugly face again?" Evonn asked enthusiastically.

"Let's forget Zorak for a while," replied Stefan. "Let's figure out what we should say to our father . . . well, our clone-father, when we find him."

Evonn thought a moment and then laughed. "How about—'Pardon me, Dr. Metvedenko, but I think I've seen you somewhere before, like every time I look in the mirror'?"

Stefan gave Evonn a disdainful look. "Metvedenko won't look the same as we do now. It was over fourteen years ago that Dr. Zorak got some of Metvedenko's skin cells at the crashed plane and cloned us. According to the newspaper article I saw, he was thirty then, so he's in his middle forties now."

Evon sighed. "I wonder how he'll react when he finds out he has two cloned sons."

"It may take some getting used to," admitted Stefan, "but I'm sure he'll help us get away from his old enemy, Zorak."

The boys fell silent, each wrapped in his private hopes and fears. Donner lay his head across Stefan's lap, and the boy scratched him softly behind the ears and down the ridges of his spine. Soon both sank into a state of lethargy.

A loud canine snore startled Stefan out of his daydreams. He glanced at his timepiece. "Evonn!" he cried, "it's time for us to get back into our crates."

Evonn smiled. "I was almost asleep. But look at Donner, Stefan. His tranquilizer has taken effect again. It seems a shame to wake him."

It wasn't easy. After several minutes of pushing and prodding, Donner finally lurched drunkenly to his feet and allowed himself to be led back to his plastic prison. Before the boys finished fastening the strap, he was snoring gently again.

Evonn leaned close to Donner's ear. "Good night, old boy, and good luck. I hope we'll be seeing you again soon."

The two boys took their sleeping pills and arranged themselves in the form-fitted crates. Before Evonn adjusted his

breathing mask, he called out, "You know what I hate most about these crates? They're too much like coffins!"

It seemed only a short time later that Evonn felt hands pulling at him, forcing liquid down his throat. He inhaled hot coffee and sat up, choking.

Where was he? His eyes focused on the wiry form of Peter Rubjak bending over him with a steaming flask. He waved it away and looked about. A man with thin, graying hair sat beside Stefan on a narrow bench. The boy smiled at him groggily.

"We're in a van," Stefan explained in answer to his brother's unspoken question.

Evonn shook himself. "Now I recognize you, Janos; how are you, Peter? Wow, I was really sacked out!"

Both men looked puzzled, then Peter Rubjak groaned disgustedly. " 'Sacked out,' " he repeated. "What is that, Evonn, more of your outdated idioms? You must have swallowed the whole set of tapes on American slang."

Janos winked at Stefan. "And this young man seems to know all the three-syllable words in the English dictionary. But that is good, Peter. They don't have the Slavic accents you and I have."

"Enough idle chatter," said Peter impatiently. "Let's get down to business. We four are going to have to split up for a while. Stefan will stay with Janos, and you with me, Evonn."

"But why?" protested Stefan. "We want to stay together."

"Look alikes attract too much attention, my boy," Janos said.

Evonn brightened. "Will we have the dog with us, Peter?" he asked eagerly.

"Dog, what dog?" Peter sounded annoyed.

"Well, uh," Evonn decided to be cautious. "I heard a baggage man read off his identification tag—'German Shepherd, owner: Peter Rubjak.' "

"Oh, *that* dog," said Peter shortly. "He won't be with us."

Evonn frowned, wondering about Peter's evasiveness. He tried to push down a feeling of apprehension as the van pulled over to the curb. He wasn't looking forward to being alone with Peter Rubjak.

2

STEFAN took long, deep breaths as he jogged around the makeshift course on the hotel rooftop. His muscles were still tight after so many hours inside the crate on the airplane.

"I feel as if I could run forever!" he called to Janos, who was waiting patiently on the sidelines.

The old man smiled. "You're looking good, my boy, but it's time to go back down."

"Already? This is the first exercise I've had in days. Aren't we safe here on the roof?"

"Perhaps," Janos replied, "but I'm expecting a communication from the others in seven minutes."

Stefan trotted to the parapet where Janos stood and toweled himself briskly. "You go ahead," he said, "I'll be with you presently."

The older man hesitated briefly and then nodded. "All right, but be quick."

Stefan sighed with relief when he found himself alone. Never in his thirteen-and-a-half years had he spent as much time in the company of others as he had in the past months. Sometimes he missed his solitary afternoons in the laboratory. It seemed to Stefan now that his life had really only begun three months ago with the sudden discovery that he was a clone. Events had moved swiftly after that—the chance meeting with his identical brother, Evonn; the escape from Dr. Zorak and the Scientific Research Station at Stovlatz; the reunion with Professor Lev and his friends; and, finally, the flight to America.

America! Stefan's heart lifted. Perhaps this huge country

could still provide sanctuary for refugees, even biological curiosities like Evonn and himself.

Stefan's eyes scanned the smog-stained concrete towers crowded against the horizon until he located the old-fashioned skyscraper where Evonn was lodged. Closing his eyes, Stefan probed that mysterious mental telegraph system he shared with his clone-brother. "Evonn," he whispered into the frosty twilight, "once we find our father, everything will be all right."

The last rays of the November sun burnished the crumbling walls of an abandoned housing project at the city's edge. Near the bend of the river, the mammoth dome that roofed the New City Plaza caught those rays and shone red-gold against the gathering shadows.

Stefan shivered and glanced at his timepiece. He had delayed too long. He pulled on his storm coat and hurried down the narrow stairs. At the door of his apartment he froze. The sounds of a scuffle came from within the room. A muffled cry from Janos was followed by a thin mechanical ping! Silence. Then something heavy thudded against the door and slid to the floor.

Stefan leaped away as if the door had suddenly become red hot. He turned and raced down the hall to the fire exit, where he threw himself against the handle. It was locked! Frantically he examined the doors to the other apartments, but they were all closed. Even the elevator indicator showed that the car was floors below. With a sinking heart, Stefan darted back toward the stairs to the roof.

A noise at the door of his own apartment warned him that someone was coming out. He would never make it up those stairs in time. Desperately, the boy dove into a small, shadowy area beneath the steps and folded his legs up under his chin.

Two burly men raced down the hall toward him, and,

without pausing, they leaped up the stairway, their shoes only inches from the boy's nose.

Stefan's mouth went dry. There could no longer be any doubt that those men were after him and that they knew exactly where to look!

Across the way an apartment door opened, and Stefan saw a cylindrical cleaning robot emerge. From its simplified back plate, he recognized it as a cheap commercial model. It glided over to a small service elevator and beamed a stop signal across the receptor plate.

As Stefan raced toward it, the robot swiveled to fix him with a blank, photoelectric stare. A metallic voice issued from its midsection.

"Can—I—help—you?"

Stefan ignored the question and darted toward the opening elevator doors.

The robot rolled forward, blocking his way. The flat voice said, "This—lift—is—designed—for—staff—use—only. Please—use—the—public—elevator—at—the—end—of—the—corridor."

Stefan checked an impulse to smash the metal creature into the wall and leap past it. But he knew that once inside the elevator, only the robot could beam in the signal to start the car again. Reluctantly he turned and took a few steps away, watching the robot intently over his shoulder. The instant it swiveled away to enter the elevator, Stefan whirled and, ducking low to avoid its eye sensors, crowded in behind it. Positioning himself at the 'blind' area at the robot's center back, Stefan moved with it to the rear of the car.

The elevator car was small. A metal stepladder stood against one wall, leaving little room to maneuver. The doors swished shut, and, as the car lurched into motion, the robot settled back on its treads, pinning the boy against the rear wall.

The air was crushed out of Stefan's lungs. By the time the

elevator bumped to a stop, his head was buzzing and bright spots danced before his eyes.

As soon as the doors opened again, the robot shifted gears and rolled off, leaving Stefan hanging onto the ladder, gasping for breath. The doors began to slide shut. Stefan leaped forward, jamming the little ladder broadside between them, and pushed himself through behind it.

He found himself in a cavernous room piled high with boxes and musty furniture. In a far corner he could see a glimmer of light. Walking toward it, he discovered that it was coming from a wide sliding door at the top of a concrete ramp. He heaved the door upward and emerged into a loading area at the rear of the hotel.

No one paid attention to the young black-haired laborer carrying a ladder down the back alley of the Calliandra Hotel.

Once he was safely out of sight, Stefan sat down weakly on the edge of a brimming trash can. Grayish plaster dust spilled down his trouser leg. Acting on impulse, Stefan scooped up a handful and streaked it across his face. 'Now those men won't recognize me,' he thought.

Not daring to waste any more time, Stefan picked up his stepladder, hooked it over his shoulder, and joined the mainstream of city dwellers hurrying home to dinner. Now another fear filled his thoughts. Had Evonn been captured? The bright lights of a communications kiosk drew his attention, and leaning his ladder against it, he searched his pockets for a token. His entire fortune consisted of ten tokens, and he dropped three into the slot. Perspiration streaked the filth on his face as he fed the numbers into telecentral. "Come on, Evonn," he urged aloud, "pick up that instrument; you must know it's me calling!"

And before its first vibration ceased, a breathless voice sounded in Stefan's ear.

"That you, Stefan?" Evonn asked, "I've been getting weird

feelings about you all evening. What's wrong?"

"Someone's after us, Evonn! They almost got me. Tell Peter to take you somewhere safe."

Evonn's voice shook when he answered. "I'm alone. Peter went out and told me to stay put until he got back."

"Forget what he told you, Evonn. Get out this minute. Don't trust a soul. Meet me at the corner of . . . uh, Seventh Avenue and Fifty-sixth Street. Go down that avenue right in front of your hotel."

"But, Stefan, are you sure? Maybe you're just getting jumpy . . ." Evonn's voice faded as some background noise drew his attention. Then, "Okay, Stefan, I'll meet you. Got to go, someone's knocking at the door."

Stefan's voice rose to a shriek. "Evonn! Don't answer that door! Hide! Get out! Run!"

Abruptly the line went dead in Stefan's hand.

THE KNOCKING became insistent. Evonn blanked the telecom and approached the door. Perhaps it was only Peter and he'd forgotten his key.

"Hey, open up, will you?" yelled a young American voice from the hallway. "I don't have all day!" The demand was punctuated by another loud thump.

"Who is there?" Evonn asked cautiously.

"Bellboy. I have an urgent message for Mr. Peter Rubjak."

Evonn moved closer to the door but made no move to open it. "I'll take the message. Just shove it under the door."

"Can't do it, friend," said the bellboy. "I was told to give it to Mr. Rubjak personally. It must be important—it came from a mobile sender, and it's in code."

Evonn frowned. "Well, Mr. Rubjak isn't . . ." he began; then, lowering his voice confidentially, he continued, "Well, listen, Peter is in the bathroom right now. And, believe me, if you wait around for him to come out, you'll be here for hours."

To Evonn's relief, the bellboy snickered and said, "I know what you mean, my old man's the same way."

"Why don't you just slide the message under the door?" Evonn repeated. "If it's in code anyway, what's the harm?"

"Wel-l, okay, but be sure he gets it, will you?"

Evonn snatched the folded paper as it emerged onto the rug. It was a computer printout made up of letters and numbers. Scattered throughout the note Evonn saw 'CL–1' and 'CL–2', the laboratory code names for Stefan and himself. Why should Peter Rubjak get a coded note from someone who still thought of Stefan and Evonn in terms of a scientific experiment? Stefan had been right; something was going on and he'd better get away fast!

Evonn snatched a tan leather jacket off the back of a chair and let himself out the side door of the suite. A glance up and down the hallway revealed only an elderly woman entering her rooms. Evonn ran directly for the stairs. By now his mind was racing well ahead of his flying feet.

'If that message came from a moving vehicle, those guys will be here any minute now. And the first thing they'll do is guard the exits. I'd better be gone by then.'

The flight of steps ended at a carpeted corridor, which Evonn followed until he came to an imposing central stairway curving down to the hotel lobby. Here he shrank behind a balustrade and surveyed the area below.

Small groups of men and women stood in the lobby and straggled in and out of wide glass doors leading to the street. Evonn merged with a family group as they walked down the stairs. Then he saw Peter emerge from behind a fluted column. Striding purposefully outside, Peter signaled a sleek black car pulling up to the curb. Four men jumped out. One jabbered angrily at Peter and pushed him. Peter shook his head and pointed upward into the hotel. They all hurried inside, each taking a different direction.

One of the four men, thickly muscled with a ruddy, pockmarked face, positioned himself just inside the doors. His restless eyes swept back and forth across the lobby.

Evonn parted from the family group when they headed for the main desk and joined several adults who were walking toward the glass doors at the right. He was almost there.

The searchlight eyes of the ruddy-faced man swung slowly toward Evonn. Quickly the boy crowded close to the woman nearest him, who was wearing a fur coat, and leaned his head familiarly against her shoulder. They passed through

the door. Then to his horror, Evonn felt the woman's body stiffen. She stopped short, pushing him away.

"Just what do you think you are doing, young man?" she asked in a shrill voice.

Evonn's face turned paprika red. He began edging away. "Oh, madam," he murmured in a heavy European accent, "please to forgive me. I have so much missed my own dear mama—she has a coat just like yours."

The woman's face softened somewhat. She turned to her companions with a shrug and they strolled off.

Evonn had felt the ruddy-faced man's eyes on him, and now he saw him make a lunge for the doors. Evonn took off like a rabbit.

The city streets were full of people. The boy dodged a zigzag path between them, trying desperately to put some distance between him and the huge man pounding after him.

Within a few blocks, the neighborhood began to change. The attitude of the people changed, too. Knots of older men lounging on the street corners turned to glower at Evonn's burly pursuer. And, as the boy began to stagger with exhaustion, he sensed that some of the strollers were silently closing ranks behind him to slow down the grim fellow who was muscling his way so rudely between them.

Out of the corner of his eye, Evonn saw a girl with stringy brown hair slyly thrust her foot into the stranger's path. With a shout of anger, the man stumbled and crashed to the ground.

Evonn didn't pause to look back. At the corner there was a boarded-off construction site. Throwing himself flat, he wriggled under the uneven fence and huddled there, breathing in huge sobbing gulps.

Out on the street, loud American voices clashed with a

furious accented baritone. After a moment the noise dwindled and the unhurried rhythm of the streets resumed again.

Evonn listened intently to discover what his pursuer would do next. At first he could make out no distinct sounds. Then his breath stopped as he heard footsteps padding along on the other side of the fence. They stopped not three meters away from him.

"HEY, KID," a young voice called through the fence, "you can come out now."

Evonn pressed his face to a crack in the boards and stared into the eyes of the stringy-haired girl he'd seen in the crowd.

"Don't worry," she said, "that big ape chasing you has gone away. He couldn't walk too well anymore. I guess he hurt himself when he fell."

Evonn dropped to his knees and squeezed under the fence again. He grinned at the girl. "That guy didn't just fall, you tripped him. Thanks, you saved my life."

"Well, he was one tough character. He knocked some little kid flat back there," she said. "Why was he chasing you?"

Evonn paused to think. "Well," he began hesitantly, "my brother and I ran away, and that big ape is trying to get us back."

"You ran away from home?"

"Oh, no," Evonn assured her. "It was a sort of orphan school in eastern Europe. We just got to this country."

"Your clothes look kind of foreign, but you speak pretty good English." She eyed him suspiciously. "Are you lying to me? Where's this brother of yours now?"

Suddenly it seemed important to Evonn that the girl believe him. He met her eyes and answered firmly. "He's waiting for me right now, want to see?"

She shook her head. "I can't, my grandmother will be wondering where I am. It sounds to me like you and your brother are in big trouble. Do you have any friends to help you?"

"No, but we'll figure something out." Evonn was anxious to get on to Stefan.

"Okay," she said, starting out to the corner. Then she turned, "Look, my name is Rosa. If you need help, wait by the New City Plaza fountain. It's near the metroliner station, and I pass it every day on the way to school."

Evonn waved briefly and hurried away. Remembering that the city was laid out in a north–south grid of numbered avenues and streets, he was able to choose an alternate route to the one he'd run before.

As he rounded the corner onto Fifty-sixth Street, a metal ladder fell across his path. Stefan's arm shot out and yanked him sideways into a doorway.

"Evonn, you made it! Am I ever glad to see you!" cried Stefan. He threw his arm across Evonn's shoulder in a tight grip.

Evonn was surprised at the depth of the feeling that shook them. Embarrassed, he looked down and rubbed his leg. "That's some crazy way you have of greeting people," he said. "What's that ladder for—besides a weapon?"

Stefan smiled. "Sorry. It fell when I reached for you. Actually, the ladder and the dirt on my face are a sort of disguise."

Evonn sobered instantly. "You were right about those men, Stefan. They came after me, too. And you know what? I think Peter Rubjak was in on the plot."

"What?" gasped Stefan. He drew Evonn back into the recesses of the store front. "Are you sure?"

"Wait till you hear! Last night after I went to bed, I heard him arguing with someone on the telecom. And then this morning he kept hovering over it. I'll bet he was waiting for a signal call. It never came, probably because you fouled up their plan by getting away."

"But, Evonn, if Peter was expecting those men, he wouldn't have left you alone!" protested Stefan.

"Yes and no. It got so late he must have known that something had gone wrong. But he couldn't call to find out with me around, listening. So he told me to stay put while he went out for something. Then, about two minutes after he left, the bellboy came up with a message for him . . ." And Evonn told Stefan about the coded note and his flight to the hotel lobby where he saw Peter Rubjak meet the four men.

When Evonn finished his tale, Stefan shivered. "It sounds like Peter is mixed up in some kind of a double cross. That coded message is the best clue we have. Who else but that fanatic Dr. Zorak would use our laboratory code labels instead of names?"

"That's what I thought," agreed Evonn. "But your old friend, Professor Lev, was so sure his group was totally loyal. How could Peter have fooled him?"

Stefan frowned. "Peter only joined us in Vienna, and that

was *after* Professor Lev had already gone back. The rest of the group accepted him, so Zorak must have arranged some kind of a cover for Peter." Stefan scanned the street in front of them nervously. "I'll tell you what happened to me later. Right now we've got to find a safer place to talk."

"Wait a minute. I want to disguise myself, too." Evonn searched the pockets of the tan jacket. In one he found a handful of all-purpose tokens and a fifty-dollar bill. A green silk scarf was in the other.

"Where'd you get the leather jacket and that scarf?" asked Stefan. "They look expensive."

"They're Peter's. I grabbed the first thing I saw when I ran out the door." Evonn ripped the scarf down the middle, twirled it loosely, and bound it around his forehead like a sweatband.

Stefan grunted in approval. "That looks casual. We should get away from here fast. Do you have any ideas?"

"Let's take a metroliner to the New City Plaza," answered Evonn, and added hurriedly, "I met a girl who lives around there. Maybe we could find her."

Stefan looked surprised but didn't stop to question him. As he moved away, Evonn heard him mutter, "Running for his life—and he meets a girl! All I found was a homicidal robot!"

The pedestrian traffic was beginning to thin out as the evening became colder. Stefan, with his ladder hooked over his shoulder, hugged the shadowy area close to the buildings. He stayed well ahead of Evonn and paused before venturing into the open or near brightly lighted stores.

Then he saw the men. They were standing in the doorway of a fast-food restaurant across the street. They were heavy, somber types, unlike the casual chattering folk about them. Neither spoke as they scrutinized the passing crowd.

Quickly Stefan ducked into the entranceway to a holomovie, where he watched the men through the right angle formed by two windows.

A moment later Evonn popped in and crouched at the far side, pretending to tie his shoe. "Are you looking at those guys across the way?" he whispered. "They're not Americans; you can tell by their clothes."

Stefan nodded. "Do you recognize them?" When Evonn shrugged, he added, "Maybe we're too suspicious. Shall we go out there again?"

"Not on your life!" Evonn rose and walked into the lobby of the holomovie.

"Wait, Evonn!" Stefan ran to catch up with him. "We'll have to buy tickets . . ."

Evonn reached into the leather jacket and held up some tokens. "This one's on Peter," he said.

Inside the darkened theater, the boys positioned themselves next to an exit within view of the single entrance door. For the moment they felt safe and immediately realized that they were famished. Evonn slipped out to the lobby and returned bearing nuts, protein bars, and fruit juice.

Stefan's eyes kept wandering away from the doorway to the glassy screens in front of them, where a noisy battle was taking place. "It's so realistic!" he whispered. "I've never seen a holomovie before, only lesson holograms."

"You're kidding!" Evonn almost choked on a handful of nuts. "Didn't you go anywhere just for fun?"

"Not really. I spent my summers working on farms and my winters studying at some scientific station like Stovlatz—not fun exactly."

Evonn was amazed. "No wonder you're shy. We boys had lots of fun at my boarding school. It's a good thing I discovered you there at Stovlatz, or you'd still be shuffling those test tubes."

"What? I was the one who found you!" Stefan whispered

indignantly. "And I made the plans to escape, and I found out about Metvedenko, too!"

"Oh yeah? Well, who masterminded the hole through the Barrier in the first place? Me! And I was the one who stole the map, and figured out about Zorak's using us to get himself political power, and . . ." He stopped abruptly. The mention of Dr. Zorak brought them both sharply back to their present predicament.

As the second showing of the holomovie neared its end, Stefan breathed out of the corner of his mouth, "We should get out of here before the lights go on. But not outside. Maybe we can find someplace to hide downstairs."

Evonn nodded. As soon as Stefan reached the lobby door, he followed. They bounded down the steps to the washroom.

The plan worked better than they expected. Evonn found that he could squeeze in behind an air duct in the men's lounge, and Stefan hid in the back of a small closet among some usher's uniforms. Not long after they were in their places, the sounds of the holomovie died away, and the boys could hear the audience leaving the theater. The place was locked up, and soon a deathly silence settled over all.

CHAPTER

5

INSIDE the airless closet, Stefan shoved aside the limp arms of light cloth jackets, which seemed to cling to him like possessive ghosts. Once in the hallway, he had no trouble finding the lounge where Evonn had hidden, for the room was flooded with light.

"Here we all are!" cried Evonn as he entered.

And as Stefan glanced about the mirror-walled room, he was greeted by a reflected multitude of black-haired boys.

Evonn's eyes widened. "Hey, Stefan, wouldn't it be creepy if there were really this many of us? It's possible, of course, we're clones."

"Oh, stop that, Evonn. We have enough problems with just the two of us." Stefan threw himself onto an overstuffed couch. "And we're going to have to solve some of them right now."

"It's hard to believe, isn't it, Stefan? Everything had been ticking along like a computer. I'd begun to think they'd just continue on that way."

Stefan shook his head. "Not me. I'm the world's greatest worrier, I guess, but even I didn't expect to run into trouble this soon. What did bother me was the lack of information about locating our clone-father. You and I will have to deal with that alone now. All we know is that after he defected, Metvedenko came to this country and is probably under the protection of the CIA. He doesn't even know we exist, no less that we're looking for him."

"Then how can we find him, Stefan? We're in a strange country without friends or even a place to stay." Evonn's voice was quavery. He coughed.

"It won't be easy," Stefan replied. "But I keep having the same dream night after night. And it always ends up with the three of us—together!"

"Yeah, I know that dream. Don't worry, I'm not going to give up yet." He yawned. "Sorry, Stefan, but I'm really beat. Before I lose it all, will you please tell me how this started? Today already seems unreal to me."

"It was real, all right!" Stefan exclaimed. "Too real for poor old Janos, I'm afraid." He clasped his hands around his knees and launched into a detailed account of what had happened.

"Wow! No wonder you sounded so upset when you called me," said Evonn. "But don't you think Janos might have been involved in that plot, too?"

"No, I'm sure those two men attacked him inside our apartment. Janos was a good old man and a close friend of Professor Lev."

"Maybe they killed him!"

Stefan winced. "Don't even say that. I doubt they'd want to chance a full-scale murder investigation. Anyway, while I was waiting for you, I called the hotel and reported hearing a fight in that room. The clerk said they'd check it out. What more can I do?"

Evonn stretched out on the carpet. "Nothing. No one can do anything more right now."

Stefan turned out the lights, feeling that he was too agitated to sleep, but it seemed only moments later that he awakened with a start. He rolled over and sat up.

What was happening? There, he heard it again—thumping noises from the theater overhead.

"Evonn!" he whispered, "wake up. I hear something upstairs."

Evonn sat bolt upright. "Whassa matter?" he croaked. Seeing his brother's intent expression, he listened, too. "Cleaning squad?" he ventured.

Stefan nodded. "It must be. They'll finish up there first, so we still have a few minutes."

In the lavatory area, Stefan hurriedly washed his face and took a long drink. "I don't hear anyone talking up there," he said to Evonn. "They must be robots."

"Tough luck, it's easier to deal with people. At least you can appeal to their sympathy or sense of humor or something."

"That's your specialty. But even I noticed a distinct lack of sympathy yesterday evening when that robot kept smashing me into the wall," said Stefan dryly.

When they reached the top of the stairs, they could see one robot busily polishing the glassy hologram screens, but the other members of the team were nowhere in sight.

Evonn gestured silently toward the street door, which was propped open with a slop bucket. They made a dash for it. Stefan snatched up his little ladder from the entryway, and they struck out for the main avenue.

A thin November sun was beginning to penetrate the smog above the city. Only a few early hour working people were on the streets, and the boys found that they, too, were headed for the nearest metro line.

Inside the underground station, Stefan and Evonn headed instinctively for the partial protection of a large free-standing map. They stood on either side of it, considering their next move.

"Hey, I only have a few more tokens, Stefan. We're going to have to find a way to exchange Peter's fifty-dollar bill soon."

Stefan stuck his head around the end of the map and gave his brother a long look. "Is that exactly honest for us to spend Peter Rubjak's money?"

Evonn sighed. "Look, the guy's a traitor. And even if it turns out that he's not, we'll find some way to pay him back."

"I guess we don't have much choice right now," Stefan admitted, turning to the map. "Where is that plaza place you spoke about?"

Evonn was busily tracing a route with his finger. "You probably never even saw a subway map before, did you, Old Test Tubes? Ah, here it is!"

No sooner had Evonn finished his sentence than a deep, recorded voice echoed throughout the station, "Double B arriving on the express track. Board now for New City Plaza and points south."

A sleek metroliner streaked down the single track and hissed to a stop. Stationing themselves on opposite sides of the car, the boys became increasingly nervous as the metro filled with passengers. Finally the recorded voice announced, "Next stop New City Plaza. The People Place of the Modern World."

When the doors opened, Stefan and Evonn were swept along in a current of business people. They soon found themselves on a moving beltway, which bore them swiftly up to the street level. Smaller arteries branched off to shop-side promenades. The boys stepped off the conveyor and stared with open admiration at the tree-lined central parkway of the New City Plaza.

"How beautiful!" breathed Stefan. "Janos told me about this place. It was originally six city blocks. Everything was renovated, consolidated, and entirely enclosed beneath a glazene dome."

"So, what's new about controlled environments?" asked Evonn, looking casually up at the clear bubble that arched above them.

"These places are usually built from the ground up, all new. But this plaza was the first effort to revitalize a sizable existing area."

But Evonn wasn't listening. His eyes were fastened on a

point several blocks away. "I think I see that fountain Rosa was talking about. Come on."

Stefan grabbed his arm as Evonn started away. "Who are you talking about?" he asked in exasperation.

Evonn removed his brother's hand. "I told you already. Some girl tripped that big ape who was chasing me yesterday."

"Why did she do that? She doesn't even know you."

Evonn shrugged impatiently. "How should I know?"

Stefan looked after Evonn and slowly shook his head.

Nothing made sense lately. He shouldered his ladder and stepped onto the conveyor.

The Plaza fountain was an imposing landmark. More than two stories high, its several powerful jets of water interwove in undulating patterns as they fell. A miniature garden of flowering shrubbery surrounded the bright mosaic catch basin.

Evonn beckoned to Stefan from an inner path, where benches had been set among the bushes. "There's a coffee shop across the way," he said. "I'm going to get us something to eat."

Stefan set down the ladder and slumped onto a bench, listening to the splashing of the fountain. Suddenly he remembered that he'd washed off the streaks of dirt that had disguised his face! He leaped up and scooped up a handful of fresh earth from the flower bed behind the bench.

The back of his neck prickled. Someone was watching him! He whirled around, poised for flight.

A brown-haired girl in a faded blue over-suit stepped toward him, smiling quizzically. "So you did come," she said. "I thought I'd run into you again. But what in the world are you doing with that dirt?"

"Who are . . ." But before Stefan finished the question, he knew.

The girl's eyes suddenly became wary. "You don't remember me at all, do you?" She began to back away.

"N-no, but wait!" he stuttered, "Yes, I do . . . but it wasn't me. Don't go away!"

CHAPTER

THE GIRL turned to run just as Evonn rounded the corner carrying a pressboard tray of food. They crashed into each other. The girl screamed as hot coffee flew across the stonework floor and sugar-coated doughnuts cartwheeled madly in all directions.

In the moment of shocked silence that followed, Stefan observed dryly, "She thought she'd run into you again."

Evonn turned to the girl with an apologetic cry, "Rosa!" he said, "you found us!"

Rosa looked back and forth from one boy to the other. Then she nodded. "Now I get it," she said to Evonn. "You're twins. You had told me you had a brother, but not that he was your twin." She stopped abruptly as a scowling plaza patrolman headed directly toward them.

"Run for it!" she warned the boys. Dropping the food she'd gathered up, Rosa dodged into the planted area.

"Halt, vandals!" shouted the maroon-uniformed patrolman, breaking into a trot.

The boys didn't need any further urging. In a flash they were across the Plaza, following the girl into a restaurant, out the back door, and into the mezzanine of a huge office building. They finally caught up to her when she paused by a brass standpipe in a marble-walled corridor.

She smiled. "Sorry, but I know that Patrol character; he's not even a real policeman. And he's a kid-hater. He's always taking our names and addresses, trying to get us barred from the Plaza. You'd think it belonged to him personally."

Stefan didn't trust himself to speak, but Evonn answered

evenly, "It's okay, we aren't too anxious for any 'names-and-addresses' routine either."

"I figured that." Rosa gave the boys a penetrating look. "We'd better go to my place and stay out of sight for a while. You two look totally shaken up. Here, stand in front of me," she ordered. "If anyone comes along, screen me."

To their surprise, Rosa inserted a key into the polished metal door behind the standpipe and opened it. Stefan half-expected to see a service elevator like the one in his hotel, but instead they stepped onto a shaky metal ladder. About fifteen feet below, two tunnels branched off into the gloom. In the dim glow of a bare electric bulb high overhead, the boys could see that the right wall of the main tunnel was corduroyed with racks of heavily insulated pipes. A stale, dank odor struck their nostrils.

"Where are you taking us?" asked Stefan.

"I told you," replied Rosa, "we're going to my place. Abuela and I—that is, my grandmother and I—live down here." Reading their astonished expressions, she stopped and faced the boys with her hands on her hips. "Look, do you guys have someplace better to go?"

Stefan thought to himself that their choices had narrowed more than ever since meeting this strange girl.

Evonn poked his brother, knowing what he'd been thinking. "We're right behind you, Rosa," he said hastily. "It's just that someone is after us, and we have to be careful."

Rosa began to walk again, throwing words back over her shoulder like a tour guide. "No one will be able to find you down here, there are miles of tunnels. They were built ages ago to carry the steam pipes to the big buildings on the street level. As long as they operate, no one bothers us down here."

"But didn't I see solar panels in that plaza dome up there?" asked Stefan. "Why are these old-fashioned steam pipes necessary?"

"Well, the scientists haven't figured all the angles yet. There's so much smog over this city the sun doesn't provide enough energy. Lucky for us, anyway!"

"How did you and your grandmother find this place?" Evonn asked, following closely on the girl's heels.

"Abuela and I came east with a whole crowd of people after the earthquake. We were the only ones in my family left alive. Mother, Father, my little brother . . . the whole house was buried in a mud slide." Her voice began to quaver and she stopped speaking.

They had reached a fork, where a smaller tunnel branched off the main one. Here in a cubicle room formed by the rusting girders of an elevator an old man dozed on a legless pink satin lounging chair.

As they approached, he sat up and eyed the boys coldly.

Rosa went over and spoke to him earnestly. He shrugged and lay down again.

Evonn looked back over his shoulder as they walked away. The old man was still watching him. "Who is he?" he asked.

"Oh, that's Mr. Franco from my home town. He works at night and sort of keeps an eye on things during the day. I'm not supposed to bring anyone down here, so I had to tell him what happened. You see, this tunnel is occupied by some of the people from my old neighborhood. Our whole area was leveled by the quake, so we left together and we've stayed together ever since."

As they continued, the boys saw signs of other living quarters. Crude rooms had been fashioned out of packing crates and draped blankets.

The tunnel took an abrupt turn to the right and, as suddenly, ended. Here Rosa stopped and spread out her hands. "This is it!" she said.

The boys could see that a valiant effort had been made to convert the dingy, dead-ended tunnel into a home. A remnant of carpeting lay on the concrete floor, and advertising posters of woodlands and wild flowers brightened the walls. At one end of the room, a packing-box table held a water glass filled with plastic roses. At the other end, a lumpy mattress was covered with a red-and-blue spread.

"I know this must look awful to you. I couldn't stand it at first either. Only bums and drifters used to stay down in these tunnels, but the city is so jammed with refugees that the whole system has broken down and people live wherever they can. Abuela is trying to save enough money to move, but it will take a long time."

Stefan shrank inwardly at the thought. He was glad to hear Evonn reply pleasantly, "It's nice and warm, and you have a real little room the way the tunnel turns here."

Rosa gave him a grateful look. "Pull up a newspaper and

sit down. Here, let's share my lunch before I go back to school."

She pulled a package out of her pocket and placed it on the box table. The boys watched intently as she unwrapped several tacos and offered them each one.

"Abuela has a vendor's cart, and she peddles these all day. If there are any left over, she tries to trade them off for other kinds of food. I help her after school. That's how we live."

Neither boy stopped munching long enough to comment, so Rosa continued her monologue. Examining their faces with open curiosity, she said, "You two are the most identical twins I've ever seen, but there's something different about the way you talk."

Stefan was amazed at the keenness of her observation. They would have to be careful with this girl.

Evonn cleared his throat. "We probably sound different to you," he explained, "because we were separated when we were babies. We went to schools in different parts of the country. Stefan majored in nuclear physics, I in political science. Although we both studied English and Chinese, my language instruction was more intensive than Stefan's."

Rosa looked puzzled. "But why were you separated? Weren't you allowed to visit one another?"

"Neither of us even knew that the other existed," Evonn said. He caught a mental wave of irritation coming from Stefan. He finished quickly. "We found each other accidentally and learned that a scientist was using us in an experiment, so we escaped. Friends helped us get to this country. But the scientist wants us back again, so his henchmen are chasing us. And that's about it."

Rosa stood up. "Well, it doesn't make much sense to me," she said. "Maybe you'll tell me more some other time."

Stefan changed the subject abruptly. "What happens about

that patrolman upstairs? Won't he be on the lookout for you?"

"He might be," she said coolly. "I'll change my clothes before I go out again. That should be enough to fool him. He's the type who thinks all kids act alike and look alike, too." She turned to Evonn. "You'd better throw away the dumb green rag around your head, though. He'd probably remember that."

Reluctantly, Evonn pulled off the silk scarf. "That's true, but Stefan and I need to look different from one another. Clo . . . twins attract too much attention."

Rosa was already rummaging through a big cardboard box. "Clotwins? We just say 'twins' over here." At that moment her eyes fell on a battered tan sportscap, which she held triumphantly aloft.

"Here is one of my best treasures! I found it on the metro track last week. It has a skid mark where the train ran over it, but it's still perfectly good. Here, take it."

Evonn grasped the cap by its visor and flipped it onto his head. "Hey, this has character! In this cap, everyone will think that I am one hundred percent native American."

Rosa smiled at him as she braided her hair. She pulled an orange shirt over her suit and was ready to go. "Maybe you two would like to explore the tunnels this afternoon," she suggested. "Only don't get lost. Just stay in the main passageway where the steam pipes are labeled. Remember the metal wall plaques marking Mercy General Hospital and the Mohawk Athletic Club?"

She laughed at the blank look on their faces.

"Before you go, Rosa," Stefan said seriously, "we'd better clear something up. Are you going to get into trouble with your grandmother if we stay down here?"

"Um—no!" Rosa thought a moment. "I'll explain about that

patrolman being so mean and, and how it was mostly my fault. Abuela will probably even let you stay for supper, since you're so crazy about tacos."

"Hey, Rosa, we have some money," cried Evonn eagerly. "It's only a fifty-dollar bill, but we don't know how to change it anyway. You take it and buy some food for tonight."

Rosa's expression became stiff. "I don't think Abuela would like that."

"Why not? We're eating your tacos. Talk it over with your grandmother after school. But remember, Stefan and I haven't had a real meal for ages and we're *starving!*"

"I get the picture." Rosa waved and promised to return soon loaded with food.

When she had gone, Evonn turned to his brother. "What's up, Stefan? Don't you like Rosa?"

"Oh, I like her, I guess; but she's such a whirlwind. Anyway, let's forget exploring these tunnels. I'd as soon catch up on some sleep."

Evonn's only reply was a mammoth yawn.

CHAPTER

7

THE MUTED rattle of pots drifted in and out of the boys' dreams, and they awoke to the aroma of food cooking. Without speaking, they lay watching Rosa and her grandmother prepare the evening meal.

A section of the asbestos insulation had been removed from around the lowest steam pipe, and now three pots sat directly on the hot metal, bubbling merrily.

Abuela, a thin little woman with white hair swept back into a loose knot, was stirring a pot of food vigorously. The fine wrinkles on her face were creased into lines of displeasure.

"Those rules are necessary for our safety, Rosa," she said in a low voice. "The boys may be nice enough; but they are strangers, and they are obviously in trouble!"

"But, Abuela, Mr. Franco was here, and the boys had no place else to go!"

"Furthermore," continued Abuela, ignoring Rosa's protest, "you know that we tunnel-people cannot afford to attract the attention of those patrolmen. We must keep our presence . . ."

Here Stefan yawned noisily and sat up on his newspaper pallet. Evonn rose to his feet. Picking up his sports cap, he said politely, "Good evening, Rosa," and, addressing Abuela, he added, "please excuse us for intruding on your hospitality this way. Allow me to introduce my brother, Stefan, and myself, Evonn."

Rosa rushed forward. "It's about time you two woke up." She giggled. "Now you sound like someone in an old movie, Evonn. Americans don't talk like that."

But Stefan noticed that Abuela's stern expression had softened considerably. He got up and joined them.

"We shouldn't have slept so long, but I'm afraid we were both exhausted. I'd like to try to explain what happened today. It really wasn't Rosa's fault."

Abuela interrupted Stefan with a firm gesture. "Yes, we will talk. But first we will eat. I hope you haven't slept away those fine appetites Rosa was telling me about. Tonight we have a small feast—chicken, rice, cabbage, and my own special jelly taco."

Stefan and Evonn reacted with an eagerness that left no doubt about their appetites.

The rectangular box had been pulled to the center of the floor and was set with an odd assortment of tableware. Two red candles cast a cheerful light on the food as Rosa brought it steaming to table.

"Why don't you just roll up your coats again and sit on them," suggested Abuela. So the clothes that had been lumpy pillows were now transformed into lumpy seats. Evonn noticed with regret that Peter's fine leather garment was becoming soiled with hard use.

When they were seated, an unexpected silence settled over the group. Stefan and Evonn reluctantly looked up from the food. Two forks clattered hurriedly back onto the table as Abuela murmured a brief prayer of thanks for the meal they were about to eat.

The home-cooked dinner, rough surroundings, and flickering candlelight gave the boys a casual holiday feeling, almost like camping out. Rosa soon had them laughing at the tale of her attempts to persuade the grocer that there was a worm in his cabbage so that he would reduce the price. Abuela told of her peddler's route and the success she'd had trading the day's left-over tacos. Then Evonn joined in with stories of secret midnight suppers in his dormitory at school.

And even Stefan admitted to having sweet-talked a farmer's wife out of an entire cherry pie.

"And this is the guy who keeps telling me how shy he is," said Evonn with a laugh.

After the last scrap had been eaten, Rosa showed the boys how to wash the dishes in a jet of steaming water from a pipe

valve. When they finished, Abuela called to them.

"Stefan and Evonn," she said, "I'm afraid we've put it off as long as we could. It's time for us to have a serious talk."

Abuela seated herself on the one rickety chair, and the boys sat cross-legged before her. Rosa hovered uneasily in the background.

"Before we begin," Abuela said frankly, "I must admit that I have been studying you both during our meal together. You're not the kind of boys I'd expect to find on the loose, even in these unsettled times. You seem well fed and well educated. Yet there is a strong scent of fear about you that worries me. Now, what kind of trouble are you in?"

Stefan knew that Evonn would be better at the explanations that lay ahead of them. He turned toward his brother with a nod.

Evonn took a deep breath and repeated much the same sketchy outline of their past that he had told Rosa earlier.

Abuela sat rigidly in her chair. Her once friendly expression became tight, and her black eyes narrowed.

"I do not believe," she said curtly, "that boys who run away from orphanages are chased all the way across the ocean simply to force them to finish school."

Stefan paled. "Please let me help to explain," he requested. "Everything that Evonn told you is true. But as you guessed, it isn't the whole story. First of all, you will have to know that Evonn and I are part of an educational experiment dealing with . . . twins. It is under the direction of a fanatic named Dr. Igor Zorak. This man doesn't care at all about Evonn and me. To him we're no different than the white mice you see caged in any scientific laboratory. When we ran away, we ruined his research experiment. He wants us back."

"I see." Abuela sat back and thought for a moment. "Although there are still gaps in your story, it seems that you aren't mixed up in anything illegal. Perhaps we should let the matter rest."

"Abuela," Stefan now appealed to her openly, "Evonn and I need a safe place to stay until we can locate a relative who is living somewhere in this country."

"A relative? I'm glad. But what about the people who brought you here; where are they?"

Stefan's face wrinkled in anxiety. "We think that one of them was injured at the hotel yesterday. The other seems to have abandoned us."

Abuela rose stiffly. Suddenly she seemed old and tired. "We are all refugees in one way or another," she said. "I can't turn you onto the streets, but I must insist that you take care of your affairs discreetly without involving us."

"That's a promise," affirmed Evonn solemnly.

Hearing this, Rosa bounded out of the shadows. "Then they can stay with us a while, Abuela?" And, as if she were afraid the old woman would change her mind, she herded the boys toward the door with a hasty, "We'd better get up to the bathrooms before it gets too late."

"Just one moment, Miss Curiosity. I have a bone to pick with you!" Abuela's gnarled hand reached out and grasped Rosa by one braid as she pranced by. She waved the boys onward, "You two go ahead; we'll catch up at the Mohawk Athletic Club turnoff."

Stefan and Evonn walked along the main tunnel in a mutual silence until Evonn broached the subject that was on both their minds. "Why didn't you tell them we are clones, Stefan? Wouldn't that have explained better why Zorak is after us?"

Stefan turned away. He rested his bent arm against the wall and buried his face in his sleeve.

"I intended to, but . . . well, I thought we'd better wait until they know us better. Clones—we're freaks, Evonn! I didn't want them to know that we are freaks."

Evonn drew a long, whistling breath through his lips. For once he was at a loss for words.

THE CLOSEST public men's room was near the metro station. It was grimy and cold inside. Standing in a blast of wind from the fresh-air vent, Evonn shivered and yanked the belt of Peter's jacket closer around his waist. He heard a ripping sound and winced with guilt. The tan leather was already dirty, and now he had torn the lining, too.

"Look here, Evonn. The water's been turned off for the night already," grumbled Stefan, looking down a row of rust-stained sinks. "We're going to have to bleed the faucets for whatever is left in them."

"I don't know how those tunnel-people can stand living like this. At night it's like some prehistoric cave down there, with the cavemen huddled around their little fires, all looking kind of scared."

"It's better than freezing in the streets," replied Stefan. "We should get up here earlier and fill Abuela's water bags." Stefan looked over his shoulder into the toilet stall Evonn had just left. "What did you drop in there?"

"Me? Nothing." Evonn strolled back in to look and let out a yelp. "Money! Look, Stefan, it's a lot!"

The boys held the bill under a bare bulb set into the wall and examined it closely.

"I can't believe it—a five hundred-dollar bill!" gasped Stefan. "Someone must have been in an awful hurry to lose this kind of money and not notice it. Maybe he'll come back for it."

"At this hour?" Evonn pushed the bill deep into his pocket as a tattered drunk lurched through the doorway. "We can't hang around here asking people if they've lost a lot of money. Let's go back."

They hurried along without speaking until Stefan stopped suddenly before a communications kiosk. "We can afford to spend a few tokens now," he said. "I'm going to call the hotel and ask about Janos."

Seeing his brother's determined expression, Evonn shrugged and squeezed in beside him.

Stefan punched out the number for the Calliandra Hotel and addressed the desk clerk in a deep voice.

"Please connect me with Mr. Janos Keplosz in room 500."

The woman at the other end of the line paused and then said, "Mr. Keplosz is no longer at this hotel. There has been an accident, and he was taken unconscious to Metropolitan Hospital. Who is this calling?"

Evonn reached out and swiftly cut off the communication.

Stefan groaned. "You heard? Poor old Janos, that proves he wasn't in on any plot against us. And now he's alone and hurt. I've got to go to him at once."

"Hold on a moment!" Evonn grabbed his brother's arm. "You could walk right into a trap. If Zorak's men left Janos alive, they did it for a reason. They hope you'll go to him, and they'll be waiting for you."

"Maybe." Stefan sagged against the kiosk.

"Look, I know how you feel," Evonn said sympathetically, "but Janos is in a hospital. He'll be well taken care of; and since he's unconscious, you couldn't even talk to him. We'll call the hospital tomorrow. Right now we should get back with this money."

He pushed Stefan ahead of him beyond a crumbling abutment and through the opening that led to the tunnels. When the boys reached Mr. Franco's cubicle, they could see Rosa waiting for them.

"What took you two so long? I was afraid you'd gotten lost."

Evonn was bursting with excitement. He grasped Rosa's elbow, and, as they walked along, he told her what had happened in a rapid-fire whisper.

Stefan followed them slowly, his thoughts still on Janos. When he reached the dead-end room, Abuela was holding the money up to the light and shaking her head incredulously.

"But what *do* you think then, Abuela?" Rosa protested. "Either you believe they found it, like they say, or you must think they mugged someone and stole that money."

Stefan looked at Evonn uneasily. Rosa had a way of going straight to the heart of a matter.

"Oh, I don't know what to think," Abuela said. "Things like this just don't happen. People don't find five hundred dollars in a subway men's room."

"Sure they do," Rosa objected stubbornly. "My teacher says that the police department in this city has a lost-and-found room with thousands of items in it."

"That's what we should do. We should turn this money over to the police," Abuela replied.

"What? The first thing they'll ask is your name and address," Rosa reminded her. "And you'd either have to explain about the boys, or why you were in the men's room!"

Even Stefan had to laugh at that. "We want you to have the money, Abuela," he said. "Evonn and I will be an extra drain on your expenses. If anything is left over, you can put it toward your savings for a better place to live."

The old woman folded her hands and thought for a moment. "That is a real temptation," she admitted, "but we can't be so selfish. What about the poor man who lost the money?"

"That's his hard luck for being so careless," answered Rosa.

"Shame on you!" Abuela shot her a reproachful look.

"Maybe we can compromise. For the time being, I'll bank the whole sum. And I know how we can find out if anyone files a lost-money complaint. If no one does, it's ours. God knows we need it!"

The next day was Saturday. Rosa went shopping with Abuela, and Stefan left to call the hospital. He met Evonn returning with the water bags. Together they entered the dead-end room.

"All they would tell me was that Janos is in a coma," he reported.

"Then there's nothing we can do yet," Evonn said. "Zorak's trained apes are really vicious, but they'll never find us now."

"Don't be so sure of that! We've got to locate our father as quickly as we can. I was thinking about Janos last night, Evonn, and I remembered something important. He mentioned a name once, a Mr. Hubert Adamson, whom he intended to contact at the CIA."

Evonn's head snapped up. "Janos told you stuff like that? All Peter Rubjak did was scowl and sharpen his body knife."

"Then Adamson is our only lead. We'd never get through to him personally if we just showed up at the CIA offices. I think we'll have to send him a letter, something to convince him that we know about Metvedenko and that we must be allowed to see him."

Evonn paced the floor. "That's not so easy. If we start talking about clones, he'll think it's a crank letter and toss it out. Why don't we simply say we're his sons . . ."

"Or better yet," broke in Stefan, "let's not even mention that there are two of us at first. And we can send a photograph with the letter."

"That's a great idea. Let's send lots of photographs; then Adamson will have to see the resemblance between us and Metvedenko. Hey, I know where there's an Insty-photo Palace on Twenty-first Street."

"Too bad we can't go together," Stefan said reluctantly.

"Try to get there Monday, and remember to remove that cap for the pictures. I wish I had an easy disguise like that, I'm tired of smearing myself with earth all the time."

Rosa and Abuela walked in loaded with groceries.

"It would be nice not to look at a dirty face every day," remarked Abuela as she plunked a bag on the table.

"Well, we *could* dye your skin red, like a red Indian," said Evonn with a wink at Rosa. "Then you'd be a 'brave' boy."

Rosa giggled. "That's a dumb pun, Evonn. But the dye idea isn't so bad. How about using some reddish hair dye? I've seen some new spray stuff that works instantly, and it would stay on until you shampoo it out."

Stefan shrugged. "It's worth a try. I'll get some later when I go up for water."

"Now what else were you two plotting when I came in? I never know what you're up to," complained the girl.

"Rosa," Abuela chided her, "you know that Stefan and Evonn have to make their own way. We have enough trouble!"

Evonn packed the last groceries in a rat-proof tin box. "Did you hear about that big fight in the far tunnels? The druggies beat up a couple of drifters who tried to move in on their territory. It's getting wild down here."

"With Mr. Franco here we're fairly safe," Abuela said. Her face broke into a glowing smile. "Oh, boys, so far there have been no reports of missing money. Maybe we can move out sooner than I thought."

Before they went to bed that night, Rosa sprayed Stefan's hair a deep chestnut color. She parted it and combed the longer hairs back over his ears.

"That makes you look older, Stefan," she cried, "and very handsome."

But Stefan caught his brother staring at him dubiously.

"In a way, I don't like it," Evonn admitted. "I sort of don't like us to look different."

"I feel that way, too," Stefan murmured. But he also felt threatening shadows creeping close about them.

EVONN clutched a brown envelope under his arm and climbed down the metal ladder. His pocket flashlight revealed only the red eyes of some rats perched on the steam pipes above him.

When he rounded the corner into the dead-end room, Stefan greeted him eagerly, eyeing the envelope.

"I got the photographs, Stefan!" Evonn opened the envelope and held up three strips of pictures of himself.

Stefan examined them critically. "They're good. Even though you're so much younger than Metvedenko, there's no missing the resemblance. Too bad you never saw that newspaper picture of him at Stovlatz."

Then Stefan handed Evonn a sheet of white paper he had been writing on. "Here's the letter I've started to Adamson."

Evonn read it quickly. "You seem to have covered everything we know about Metvedenko—military hero, academic titles, scientific research, defection, the plane crash where he lost the little finger on his right hand, and his presence here under CIA protection. That should convince them that we know too much to be ignored."

"Now what shall I write about your photographs?" Stefan asked.

Evonn knelt beside his brother. "Tell them that the boy in the pictures is Metvedenko's son and that he'll visit the CIA offices here on January fifteenth. That will give them enough time to get their act together."

"They have no reason to trust you," said Stefan. "But if you get into trouble, I'll find a way to get you out."

"Trouble? I'm only asking for a chance to talk to Met-

vedenko personally." Evonn shook his head. "After all, we're dealing with the CIA, not the KGB! But," he added in a subdued voice, "I am glad you'll be here to back me up."

Stefan sealed the envelope. "We can't trust this letter to the regular mails, Evonn. I'll take it over to the CIA building right now and simply leave it with the receptionist. It won't take long, so don't worry."

The moment Stefan was out of sight, Evonn began to worry. He hadn't expected Stefan to dash off like that. Within an hour Evonn was pacing back and forth on the subway platform. A patrol dog sensed his agitation and growled as the boy passed by. Disgusted with himself, Evonn returned home.

Inside the tunnel he passed Rosa and Abuela visiting with Mr. Franco.

"Where's your brother?" Rosa asked. To his distress, she accompanied him back to the room.

"What is the matter with you, Evonn?" she demanded. "You're as jumpy as a one-whiskered rat. I only asked where Stefan went."

Evonn spun around. "What we do is none of your business. Just leave us alone, will you?"

Rosa shrank back as if she had been slapped. "If *that's* the way you feel, I'll never speak to you again. You and your big, important secrets, I hate you!" She turned on her heel and stamped out.

Evonn hurried after her. "Wait Rosa, I'm really sorry. I only lost my temper because I'm so worried. Come back and I'll try to explain."

"There you go again, you're *so worried!* There are millions of twins in this world. Why should that Dr. Zorak bother to chase you two around forever?"

Evonn flushed. "Because we're not just twins—we're *clones!*"

Rosa gasped. "Clones?" she repeated wide-eyed. "But you and Stefan seem like real—like regular people to me."

Evonn winced. He turned back to their cubicle with Rosa close behind him.

"I didn't mean that the way it sounded!" she cried. "I've only heard about cloning in connection with agriculture and medicine. Aren't clones sort of artificial?"

Evonn sighed. "Well, it's kind of technical to explain, but I'll make it short. Life normally begins with a fertilized egg cell. A clone's life begins with a cell from anyplace in the body. Stefan and I were grown from skin cells taken from the finger of a man named Grigory Metvedenko. We never had ordinary parents. It was all done in a laboratory."

Rosa was amazed. "Then you two are younger copies of Metvedenko," she said, "and exact replicas of one another; but you and Stefan aren't *exactly* alike."

"That's because outside influences in our environment were different—life style, nutrition, accidents, disease."

"Why did Dr. Zorak want to clone *people*, Evonn? The world is already too crowded."

Evonn managed to answer Rosa calmly. "We think it was done for revenge. Our father, Metvedenko, walked out on Zorak's government project and left him looking like a fool. When Metvedenko's escape plane crashed, he got away; but Zorak found that Metvedenko's finger had been severed. That's when Zorak began his great scheme. He couldn't have the man himself, but in time he could have his clones. And through them, political power. Stefan and I were being educated especially to his purposes!"

"Now I understand. But that's plain rotten!" Rosa collapsed onto a cushion. "Why didn't you tell us about this before, Evonn?"

Evonn was too tired to evade the question. "Stefan doesn't want you to know we're clones. He's afraid you'll think we're freaks."

"Oh-h, poor Stefan! Does he think I care what happened when he was only a drop of protoplasm?"

"Look, Rosa, Stefan was raised mostly by himself, working his brains out in some lab. He's uneasy about what people will think of him. You can't really blame Stefan . . ."

"Can't blame me for what?" Stefan exploded into the room. "What are you saying about me? Did you tell about the CIA, Evonn?" He regarded his brother intently, then an expression of hurt amazement crossed his face. "You told Rosa about . . . us! You knew I didn't want her to know!"

"Hey, what's the matter with you, Stefan?" cried Evonn. "I'm a clone, too, remember? Only I don't happen to think of myself as a freak."

Rosa walked around Stefan to face him directly. "Look, I'm

sorry you're upset," she said, "but there are too many secrets around here. I can understand that you don't like being a clone, Stefan. I don't like being an orphan either. But I have Abuela, and I have you two for friends. I don't care about your stupid genes!"

Stefan swallowed hard. Then he smiled and said, "Well, if you don't care, Rosa, why should I?"

A large tear rolled down from one of Rosa's eyes, giving her elfin face an oddly comic look.

"Boys," she said quietly, "I really care about you, and I'm so afraid that some day you two will disappear and I'll never even know what happened. Can't you tell me what you are doing with the CIA?"

"It's not that we want to keep secrets from you, Rosa," explained Stefan, "but there could be trouble and Abuela doesn't want you involved."

"Tell you what, Rosa," suggested Evonn, "if you promise not to interfere, we'll tell you as much as we safely can."

Rosa agreed instantly. "I won't interfere, I just want to know what you're trying to do."

Evonn told her quickly about the packet of photographs and the letter. Then turning to Stefan, he said, "Now, tell us what happened when you went to mail the envelope."

"Actually," Stefan admitted, "it wasn't at all exciting. A guard stopped me the minute I stepped inside the CIA building. He took my package, slid it through a sonic security device, and dropped it in the mail chute. So . . . I came home again."

Evonn frowned. "Then you didn't find out anything that will help me on January fifteenth?"

"What do you mean by that?" cried Rosa, turning on him. "You can't go there. They'll know who you are by then!"

Both boys glared at her.

"Oh," she murmured. "I wish you could just handle it all

by mail. Anyway, the fifteenth is my birthday. I was hoping we could all have a party. With a cake and candles—you know, like a family."

"We'll be there," promised Evonn.

". . . if at all possible," added Stefan.

The night of January fourteenth was a sleepless one for both boys. Stefan tried to fasten his mind on the next evening's birthday festivities, but his thoughts kept returning to the ordeal Evonn would face at the CIA in the morning. Finally he whispered into the darkness.

"Want to call it off, Evonn? Maybe we can find a better way."

"Not a chance!" came the reply. "Our entire lives have been leading up to this day!"

THE TOWERING government buildings sat on a snow-covered rise surrounded by rows of winter-barren maple trees. As Evonn mounted the broad stone steps to the CIA offices, a sense of foreboding crept over him. 'This is a fool's errand,' an inner voice warned him. 'If the CIA doesn't believe you, they'll think you're crazy. And if they do, you may not get out again!'

Lift and step, lift and step. Evonn's feet ignored the battle within his mind. At the top of the steps, the heavy doors opened slowly. A gray-uniformed guard stepped forward to block Evonn's way.

"I am Evonn Radescu . . ." An icy sweat broke out under the boy's arms. "I am Evonn Radescu Metvedenko," he blurted. He waited, expecting the guard to wave him away.

But the guard looked down at a printed card and nodded. "Straight down the hall," he said, "room 105."

Evonn felt the blood drain from his face. Again, it was his feet that carried him forward—down a corridor, through the door, and into a green room. Even the rug and drapes were green. The reception desk was studded with communications equipment—word processors, telecoms, and TV units. As Evonn approached the young woman behind the desk, she hastily blanked out a message on the screen before her and rose to her feet.

"I am Evonn Radescu Metvedenko," he said.

Her eyes shifted sideways to the screen. "Yes," she said. "Come with me." The young woman led him down a short flight of stairs toward the back of the building. She ushered him into a small room and excused herself.

Evonn was suddenly alone. He looked around nervously. At the far end of the room, two low molded chairs faced a sturdy desk. There were no papers, books, or electronic hardware of any kind to be seen. Three splashy paintings were grouped on the wall behind the desk; otherwise the room was bare.

Evonn began to fidget. The quiet was getting on his nerves. Not even the noise from the other offices could be heard. He began to take off his leather jacket but stopped midway. No telltale stains of perspiration should betray his anxiety. He walked to the windows, gazing longingly outside. The thin rays of winter sun revealed a crisscross pattern of hair-thin threads imbedded into the composition glass, like tiny bars. A feeling of panic gripped him as he searched in vain for pulls or levers to raise the window. But it was sealed!

Before he could move away, the door behind him opened and two men entered. The taller of the two, a solemn individual with light sandy hair, strode to the seat behind the desk. The other remained standing near the door. Evonn received only a fleeting impression of a tanned fellow of middling height with a vigorous mane of gray-white hair and tinted glasses.

The sandy-haired man beckoned Evonn to take a seat. "I am Mr. Adamson and this is Mr. Griggs," he said.

Evonn acknowledged the introduction with a slight bow. "I am Evonn Radescu Metvedenko."

An unnerving silence followed. Evonn sat down on one of the chairs facing the desk. Mr. Griggs sat in the other chair, slightly behind him. Finally, Mr. Adamson spoke.

"Now, youngster, what do you want of us?"

Evonn was appalled at the question. These men were placing the entire burden of the interview on him. Suddenly he felt foolish.

"Last week . . ." A shrill voice that Evonn scarcely recognized as his own repeated the phrases he had practiced so many times before with Stefan. ". . . you received in the mail a packet containing photographs of me and some very confidential information about Dr. Grigory Metvedenko. That was to convince you of the truth of what I am about to tell you. I need your help in contacting Dr. Metvedenko. I am his son."

The man behind Evonn barely managed to choke off some kind of an exclamation. Mr. Adamson leaned forward abruptly.

"Do you mean," he snapped, "that you have involved the CIA in this ridiculous exercise merely to locate an absent parent? I suggest you try the Bureau of Missing Persons."

Evonn was stunned. "Listen to me!" he cried. "Dr. Metvedenko defected to this country thirteen years ago. You are the only means I have of reaching him. Professor Lev told us that he will have a different name by now and a whole new personal history as well. Please, you must take me to him; he's the only one who can really identify me. Tell him that Dr. Zorak is after me and I need help!"

Evonn stopped. This was just the sort of hysterical admission that he and Stefan had decided against. The CIA was only to lead them to Metvedenko; the rest was for his ears only. Gradually he became aware that the atmosphere in the room had changed. It crackled with tension. Mr. Adamson's gaze was locked fiercely with that of the other man.

Mustering what small amount of nerve he had left, Evonn stood up. "Mr. Adamson," he said, "I came here to request cooperation from the CIA. I can see now that I'm not going to get it, so I think it best if I just leave." His hurried stride toward the door was interrupted by a commanding gesture from Mr. Adamson.

"Not so fast, youngster. What is all this about a defector with a new name and a new identity? I think perhaps the CIA should have a few answers from *you!*"

Evonn reluctantly returned to his chair. Now he would have to watch his step!

Mr. Adamson walked around to the front of the desk and sat on the corner nearest Evonn. He nodded to Mr. Griggs, who rose and pressed some buttons in the rear of the room. Several down-lights flashed on, bathing Evonn in a harsh glare.

"You will please give us a complete statement of personal statistics," said Mr. Adamson in an ominous voice, "including name, address, parents' names, place of birth and/or date of entry into this country."

Evonn stiffened. He was well-prepared to answer questions, but this was obviously an official interrogation. To his surprise, Mr. Griggs now positioned himself beside Adamson at the desk. He gave Evonn a reassuring smile and took over the questioning. Whenever Evonn's gaze wandered away from the two men, it was brought back immediately by sharp comments from Mr. Adamson. Suddenly Evonn realized why—he was being filmed! The camera must be located behind the desk, disguised in one of the paintings.

Once again Mr. Adamson interrupted. "You say that you were born and educated in the Bihor foothills—on what date, then, did you enter this country?"

Evonn's answer elicited a satisfied grunt from the sandy-haired Adamson, and the inquisition abruptly came to an end. Both men walked to the door. Mr. Adamson turned to warn Evonn that he was to wait.

As soon as the door closed behind them, Evonn tiptoed over to it. Hearing nothing, he gingerly grasped the knob and the door swung open.

A muscular young man leaning against the wall outside looked at him with heavy-lidded eyes.

"Going somewhere?" he asked.

"Oh, no," said Evonn. "Just looking around."

A few minutes later, Mr. Adamson returned alone. Evonn

had a vague feeling that he had somehow lost an ally. With a self-congratulatory smirk on his face, Adamson seated himself behind the desk.

"And so, youngster," he said, "we discover, just as I thought, that you are a liar. And not a very clever one at that. Item one: No passport in your name has ever been processed at a port of entry in this country. That fact, plus your flawless English, label you as a native-born American." He waved aside Evonn's attempted protest. "Item two: The 'confidential' information you revealed about your mysterious Dr. Metvedenko is public knowledge to anyone who cares to avail himself of back issues of any European free press."

Evonn stared at the man dumbfounded. Adamson hadn't believed one word that he had said.

"There have been a number of attempts in the past," Adamson continued, "to undermine the power and prestige of the CIA. Any further attempt on your part to charge this agency with responsibility for the disappearance of foreign personnel will cause instant retaliation. The CIA now has a complete dossier on you, young man, and it is on file."

Mr. Adamson rose and leaned across the desk toward Evonn. "I can only assume that someone has put you up to this. If you weren't under the legal age, I would certainly detain you for further questioning. Here's a bit of advice: Get out of here and don't ever let me see your face again."

A few minutes later a thoroughly confused Evonn found himself outside. How good the cold air felt in his lungs; how sparkling the snow crust that rippled across the buried lawns; how sweet the taste of freedom!

"SOMETHING is wrong, Evonn," said Stefan. "Adamson's whole reaction sounds fake." Stefan had materialized unexpectedly from a doorway only two blocks north of the government buildings, claiming that he hadn't been able to bear the long wait at the tunnels.

Now his face was taut with distress. "They're up to something, Evonn. If the CIA had no interest in Metvedenko, Adamson would never have bothered to have a personal meeting with you. That little scene was too slick!" He glanced over his shoulder. "Get that cap back on your head and let's get away from here."

They walked for several blocks. The sun disappeared behind a dingy layer of clouds, and the wind gushed forth from behind a row of warehouses, blasting them with grit at every side street.

Stefan, hurrying in the lead, slackened his pace so suddenly that Evonn collided with him from behind. He jerked Evonn around the corner of the building into an alley. "Do you hear that?" he whispered.

Evonn found it hard to concentrate; he was too drained to care. Then he heard it—the measured crunch of feet running along the snow-crusted sidewalk behind them.

With the renewed shock of fear came a powerful need to see who was following them. But before Evonn could move, Stefan whispered, "No! If he were a friend, he'd have called out to us." Once more he dragged Evonn after him.

Small dragon-puffs of vapor issued from Stefan's nostrils as he scanned the deserted street at the top of the alley. On both sides, warehouses loomed against the dull skies like barred fortresses.

"We've got to hide," panted Stefan. "We can't get . . ."

A crunching sound near the entrance to the alley behind them propelled the boys forward. "Over there!" Evonn pointed across the way to a blocked-off subway entrance. Its locked iron gate hung loose at the hinges and a plank in the boarded door behind it had been torn away, revealing pitch blackness within.

The boys dashed down the steps and squeezed through the narrow opening. Reeking cold air enveloped them. Stefan tripped over a mound of trash just visible in the crack of daylight—a few rags, a lantern, empty food containers— all evidence that even this dismal cave was used as a refuge.

Evonn had already moved ahead into the murky recesses. "Come on!" he urged. "We've got to go farther in. Just keep running your fingertips along the wall like I'm doing."

Stefan groped his way after Evonn and soon his fingers came in contact with the familiar leather jacket.

Evonn turned. "This rotten wall ends here and I can't tell what's in front of us. Do you think we can risk using a flash-light?"

Stefan held his breath. No noises reached them from the street above. "We'll have to risk it, but just for a second." He used his body to shield the powerful beam of the small electric torch.

Evonn sucked in his breath. "Wow, did you see that? The pit for the metro track is right in front of us."

Ka-boom! A cannonlike report of splintering boards sent shock waves throughout the concrete chamber behind them. Without a word, Stefan and Evonn joined hands and leaped into the abyss at their feet.

The blind drop ended with a jolt that rattled the boys' teeth. Evonn was hauled to his feet by Stefan, and together they crept into the black cavern guided only by the narrow length of the metro track.

After an eternity of stumbling, Stefan felt Evonn's hand drag and realized that he had stopped to look back.

"No one would follow us any farther," he whispered. "Maybe we don't have to go on."

Suspended in inky space, they waited. For a moment they could hear only their own labored breathing. Then a dull thud reverberated along the track bed, followed by a high-pitched yelp and a deeper voice cursing.

"They fell off the platform. Oh, I hope they broke their legs." Evonn's voice lifted. "I'm sure they have no lights; they'll have to give up!"

"Hush!" Stefan yanked hard on Evonn's hand. "I think they're coming!"

A loud-voiced man seemed to be ordering another to go ahead. Soon the boys heard scratching noises and the creaking of uncertain feet moving along the track.

Reluctantly, they set off again. "This is crazy," protested Evonn. "What are our chances in here? We'll either fall into a hole somewhere or be squashed flat by a metroliner!"

"What do you think our chances are if we turn back now?" countered Stefan. "Anyway, the next metro station can't be far away. We will surely be able to get out there."

Evonn struggled along silently for several minutes, then he said, "Stefan, the track seems to be curving off to the left. If there's a fork ahead, we're in luck. I know a way we can lose those guys. Wait here."

He was gone only a moment and returned jubilant. "There is a fork," he exclaimed, "and I laid my cap beside the track that branches off the main line. I'm sure those guys will find it when they're feeling around for a clue to see which way we went. Maybe we'll lose them!"

Gradually the stealthy sounds of pursuit became fainter. "I think your trick worked, Evonn." Stefan sounded hopeful.

They began to move along at a faster rate. Then Evonn yanked Stefan's sleeve again. "Hey, I can *see* you, Stefan! It's getting lighter ahead."

Almost imperceptibly, the murky gloom receded. The boys could make out rough-hewn walls on either side of the track. Then, rounding a bend, they were brought up short at the eerie sight that met their eyes.

A multi-level exchange station with a broad upper promenade and an elaborate system of crosswalks had been started but never completed. Dust, cobwebs, the debris of years festooned the remains of forsaken grandeur. Over all arched a mammoth ceiling of a pearly yellowish translucent material through which patterns of shifting light bathed the arcades below. As the boys stared, awestricken, an oblong shadow of a boat drifted overhead, almost blotting out the light. A fog horn wailed forlornly in the distance.

"That must be the East River up there!" gasped Evonn, "I wonder why this fantastic underwater project was abandoned before it was finished."

But Stefan was almost weeping with disappointment. "We can't get out, Evonn. This place is closed off like a tomb. Look at those staircases—they end in midair!"

Again the fog horn sounded a hollow warning.

Stefan's eyes narrowed as another thought occurred to him. "If that's the East River up there and we're traveling on a main line, it's sure to intersect with one of the cross-town metro lines. They're the busiest in the city. It's worth a try."

They joined hands and reluctantly shuffled deeper into the abandoned subway. The roadbed began a long, gradual descent, and the air became clammy.

A tiny, icy pain darted suddenly down Stefan's back. With a cry he clapped his hand over the spot. It came away wet.

"What's the matter?" Evonn's frightened voice penetrated the gloom.

"Dripping overhead!"

"Strange. I was just noticing how slippery everything has become," Evonn observed.

They proceeded with caution until Evonn, in the lead, shouted aloud as both boys plunged ankle deep into freezing water.

"What the . . ." Stefan turned on his pocket flashlight briefly. The boys saw tiny wavelets at their feet rippling onto a flooded track bed.

"Washout! We've got to go back!"

Clinging to the track for balance, the boys slipped and slid back up the muddy roadbed. As soon as Evonn reached drier ground, he turned. "Come on, Stefan," he called, "it's better up . . ."

Evonn stopped abruptly, for out of the darkness footsteps pounded toward them and a sharp command rang out. "Attack!"

Stefan's flashlight dropped from his hands as a blur of gray fur and fangs hurtled toward him.

"Watch out!" cried Evonn. As he spoke, a wiry human figure leaped on him, driving him face down into the icy slime. Evonn twisted his head to the side; and, in the powerful beam of the fallen flashlight, he saw the sneering face of Peter Rubjak.

"At last I've got you, you little thief!" Peter raged. "You almost ruined me, but Zorak knew you'd be stupid enough to show up at the CIA sooner or later."

Evonn lashed out with his feet, but the small man drove his knee between the boy's legs and, with a quick twist, turned his arm back at the elbow.

"Oh, no you don't!" he panted. "You're not getting away from me again. Not when I've got my money right here under my fingers. Thoughtful of you to wear my jacket tonight, it makes things even easier."

Sick with pain, Evonn watched Peter reach into his belt and draw out his long knife. The blade flashed in his hand.

"Drop that knife!" A new voice boomed out of the void and a lantern bobbed toward them.

Peter's upraised hand swiveled, and he threw the knife in the direction of the lantern. Then his fist swung down against Evonn's temple.

Bright sparks flickered along the boy's nerve ends, and he felt himself drop into oblivion.

12

Climbing back along the track, Stefan had heard a man shout and then Evonn's warning cry. But before he could move to see what was happening a lightning bolt of fur and sinew struck him in the chest, knocking him over backward. Yellow-green eyes gleamed above him and a hot gust of animal breath bore down on his jugular vein. Then suddenly, unbelievably, the boy felt a warm tongue frantically licking his face and ears. The large beast standing over him whined with joy and butted his head into Stefan's shoulder.

A thrill of recognition penetrated Stefan's paralyzed brain. "Donner?" he cried.

An answering bark and an enthusiastic nudge caused Stefan to feel weak with relief.

"Oh, Donner, it's you! Good boy, you remember me."

In the background Stefan could hear Peter Rubjak's voice, raving in anger. Someone shouted. A lantern appeared out of the gloom and then clanked to the ground. Sounds of a struggle echoed throughout the dark cavern.

"Sit, Donner, sit, good old fellow! You've got to let me up," he whispered.

Reluctantly the big dog moved aside and sat, watchful eyes never leaving Stefan's face.

For several minutes Stefan couldn't make sense out of what was happening. Silhouetted against the light from the lantern, two men were locked in hand-to-hand combat. They were grappling over an object one held outstretched. It was a gun.

With a mighty wrench, the bigger man broke the other's hold. He swung the gun against his opponent's ear and barked, "No more! Get down flat on your stomach and don't make any sudden moves. It's too dark in here for me to take any chances. One move and you're dead!"

Stefan shrank back into the shadows. Who was the man holding the gun on Peter? His profile reminded Stefan of someone he had seen before, and yet . . . Stefan decided he was mistaken. This man with the thick mane of gray-white hair was a stranger.

As if sensing Stefan's eyes on him, the man shot a quick glance in his direction. "Now, call off that dog!" he said sharply to Peter.

Instantly Peter raised his head and shouted, "Attack, Donner! Get the gun!"

Donner crouched, the coarse hackles along his back bristling. Stefan threw both arms around the dog's neck and dragged him back.

"Down, Donner!" he cried. "Down, I say. Sit!" To Stefan's surprise, the knotted muscles in the animal's powerful hind legs relaxed; but Donner remained standing, funnel ears pricked forward.

At Peter's first outburst, the stranger had jabbed the muzzle of his gun forward against his mouth. Peter took the hint and said no more.

"Good work with that dog," said the stranger, nodding at Stefan approvingly. "Your friend is lying over here to my left. He's been knocked out. When the dog's calmed down, get the lantern and take a look at him."

The man frisked his prisoner with his free hand and drew a length of nylon cord from under Peter's coat.

"Ah-ha! I wonder who you planned to use this on," he said. "Well, it will do just fine for you."

Stefan watched curiously as the stranger, still working with one hand, wrapped several lengths of cord around Peter's wrists and ankles. Quickly he reached forward and shoved a scarf into the little man's mouth. Only then did he place the gun close by on the ground while he knotted the rope tight.

Stefan stroked Donner gently until he felt the dog relax. Then together they crept over to Evonn's side.

The sight of his brother's form lying motionless on the ground turned Stefan's legs to rubber. He knelt and lay his head against Evonn's chest. The steady beating of the young heart under Stefan's ear broke the boy's last reserve of strength. He pressed his face into Donner's warm fur and sobbed.

The stranger appeared at Stefan's side. He placed a sympathetic hand on his shoulder. "Don't worry, he'll be fine."

He ran his fingers lightly across Evonn's neck, checked his pulse, and nodded, satisfied. "Let's get him out of here."

Simultaneously they both reached to lift Evonn's inert body. The stranger shot Stefan a quick glance and then said tactfully, "You'll need to lead the way with the lantern. I can carry him."

Stefan nodded. "But what about Peter Rubjak?" he asked.

"So you know him. Obviously you know the dog," he said. "I've radioed for a squad to come in and pick him up." The man pointed to a portable communicator strapped to his belt. "Evidently there were just the two of them; this Rubjak and the German shepherd."

"What happens to Donner now?"

At that the dog, who had been watching them anxiously, pressed against Stefan's side.

"Shoot him!" screamed Peter, spitting the end of the scarf out of his mouth. "He's vicious and untrainable. He's a traitor!"

But Stefan had already discovered numerous half-healed welts on Donner's head and back. He knew that cruel treatment had been a daily part of the dog's life.

"This animal is more loyal than you'll ever know. You are

the one who is the vicious traitor!" He picked up the lantern. "Donner can come with us, can't he Mr. . . .?"

"Of course he can. And my name is Griggs, Malcolm Griggs," the man responded. "I'm working with the CIA."

Stefan digested that news silently, deciding that this was no time to question an ally. He said, "Mine is Stefan."

Together they set off down the tunnel. This time a soft circle of yellow light preceded them. Now that the crisis was past, Stefan found that he was trembling, and it was all he could do to hold the lantern steady.

There was little conversation between the exhausted boy and the man Griggs. Although obviously younger than his white hair indicated, he was straining to carry Evonn's sagging body over the uneven track bed. Donner pranced along at their side, seeming to sense that they were on the way outside again.

Soon they could see the glare of electric torches bobbing along the track toward them. Two men called out to greet Griggs. As they approached, one made a move to take Evonn from his arms.

"No!" Griggs ordered, "You go get Peter Rubjak. I'll handle this situation myself. No interference, please."

They set off again. Mr. Griggs stumbled but regained his balance immediately. "I don't understand how you were able to find your way down here without lights," he said. "Have you been here before, Stefan?"

"No, but Peter had the dog to lead him. Donner was just following our scent. As for Evonn and me, it *was* almost impossible—but there's a certain sense of space you develop when you've been underground as much as we have lately."

Stefan winced, wondering if that had been wise to say. He changed the subject.

"What are you going to do with us when we get up to the streets, Mr. Griggs?"

"That depends on Evonn's condition and what I find out about you two and Peter Rubjak."

Stefan was in no mood to be tactful. "And that, Mr. Griggs, depends on what *I* find out about *you!*"

The man beside him made a strangled noise somewhere between a startled laugh and an exclamation of annoyance.

They passed the fork in the tracks, and before long Stefan could smell the urine-drenched atmosphere of the abandoned station where they had started out. As he ducked through the shattered entranceway, the clean, brisk air affected him like a sweet midsummer's breeze. His flagging spirits lifted, and he felt that all things were yet possible.

At the top of the steps a man in a dark coat stepped forward. "Griggs?" he asked.

"Yes, I have the boys. Please help me carry this one to the car. I'm in a hurry."

The man scooped Evonn up and carried him to the first of two black limousines parked a discreet distance away. He deposited him carefully on the back seat. Stefan crawled in next to Evonn and, like an unobtrusive gray shadow, Donner squeezed by and curled into a ball on the floor.

Through the front window of the car, Stefan saw Mr. Griggs arguing with the other man. Finally, Griggs shrugged and they both walked back to the car.

At that moment Stefan felt a twitch at his sleeve. Startled, he glanced down at Evonn. His brother's eyes were wide open. Stefan placed a warning hand over Evonn's mouth. Mr. Griggs opened the passenger door and the other CIA agent jumped into the driver's seat.

As the powerful automobile pulled away from the curb, Stefan looked up quickly to see if the door beside him had been locked.

CHAPTER

13

"WHERE are you taking us, Mr. Griggs?" asked Stefan. A quick glance assured him that the car doors had not been locked.

"We're taking Evonn to the hospital," Griggs said. "He's had some hard blows to the head, and we can't take a chance on a fracture."

The driver, a tall, bald-headed man, nodded in agreement.

A hospital! That could be a kind of imprisonment. Yet he couldn't argue against medical care. "Okay," he said aloud, trying to sound confident, "on two conditions. One, that I choose the hospital, and two, that Evonn be entered as 'name unknown' on the register. He'll probably be too groggy to answer questions anyway." Stefan nudged Evonn meaningfully.

Stefan saw a smile flicker across Mr. Griggs's reflected face.

"I hardly think you're in a position to bargain, Stefan. However, in exchange for some answers from you, I'll try to accommodate your wishes. You do understand that we're going to have to let the doctors decide what's best for your friend."

"He's not just my friend, Mr. Griggs," Stefan said quietly, "Evonn is my brother."

Mr. Griggs jerked his head around and stared directly at Stefan. "I see," he said in a strained voice, "with all that mud on your face, I missed the resemblance. Are you twins?"

"Well, yes . . ." answered Stefan.

"All right then, Stefan, do you know a hospital for your brother?"

Stefan racked his brains to remember the name of the hospital he'd seen engraved on the brass wall plate near the main tunnel. At least there they'd be close to home.

"Mercy Hospital," he said, "that's it, Mercy General Hospital."

"I know where it is," the driver assured them. "It's just beyond New City Plaza."

They pulled up to the emergency entrance, and Donner was left behind to guard the car. Two orderlies quickly brought a stretcher, and Evonn, accompanied by Griggs, was wheeled to an examining room.

Stefan paced the floor of the waiting room in an agony of suspense. What was happening? Was Evonn alert enough to handle the situation? Finally a nurse came in and motioned to Stefan.

"Are you Stefan?" she asked. "Come with me, please."

"How is . . . how is my hurt friend?" Stefan stammered.

"He has just come out of sonar, where his skull was scanned for injury. He seems fine, although he's still unable to tell us much about himself or what actually happened."

She handed Stefan a visitor's pass and added disapprovingly, "You're almost as muddy as he was. You can clean up upstairs. Mr. Griggs insisted that the boy have a private recovery room while the doctors are reviewing his test results."

When Stefan entered room 405-A, he found Evonn freshly washed, lying back against a mound of pillows. He had a bandage around his head, and his eyes were closed. Mr. Griggs sat on a chair next to the bed, studying the boy's face anxiously.

Evonn's eyes fluttered open as Stefan approached his bed. "Stefan!" he said thickly, "I was so afraid they wouldn't let you up here. There's something you should know about Mr. Griggs. He's with the CIA. I saw him there this morning."

Stefan nodded. "He told me, Evonn. He was following

you; that's how he came to save your life—both our lives, I guess." He turned to the man beside the bed. "Thank you, Mr. Griggs. I don't know what the CIA will do with us now, but please don't separate us!"

Mr. Griggs coughed. "An awful lot has happened today that I don't understand, Stefan; but you must believe me when I tell you that I am your friend. As for Evonn, I'm recommending milk and raspberry tarts. As for you, if you would like to join us, get into that bathroom and remove a few layers of mud. Then we'll talk."

Inside the bathroom, a wild man looked back at Stefan from the mirror. He washed vigorously and tried to smooth back the long locks that drooped around his ears. He wet the bar of soap and ran it over the surface, pasting the hair in place.

As he was re-entering the room, he heard Mr. Griggs saying to Evonn, ". . . behind bars for years. He'll be faced with charges of assault and battery, possession of deadly weapons, resisting arrest, and probably some kind of passport irregularities."

He looked up at Stefan. "We're talking about Peter Rubjak," he said. "Come and join us, the tarts have arrived."

The aroma of hot fruit pastries instantly improved Stefan's outlook on life. He sat next to the man at a small table set beside the bed.

"Oh, you've been hurt, too!" cried Griggs. He leaned over and blotted the back of Stefan's neck with his napkin. He stared at the reddish stain and then said slowly, "This isn't blood . . ."

". . . it's hair dye." Stefan finished the sentence for him. "Sorry, Evonn, I should have known better. I put some wet soap on my hair, and I guess the dye started to run."

"Hair dye?" Mr. Griggs frowned. "What is going on here? First, one boy shows up at the CIA claiming to be Metvedenko's son. Then a twin brother appears in disguise. You two have a lot of explaining to do."

Evonn sat forward on his bed. "You know what happened when I went to the CIA this morning, Mr. Griggs. I tried to get them to help us, but instead they said I was a trouble-maker and threw me out. Now you suddenly show up again. What reason do we have to trust *you?*" Evonn lay back against the pillows, holding his aching head.

"I can see your point, Evonn," said Mr. Griggs seriously. "We're both going to have to take some chances. To make it fair, I'll begin. I work for the CIA, as you know, but only on special assignments. I'll tell you both frankly that when Evonn's package arrived last week, the agency was thrown into a turmoil. Almost all the information you gave us was confirmed in our computer banks. And the resemblance be-tween the photos of Metvedenko and Evonn is remarkable. But the CIA needed to know more. That's when I was called in. You see, I'm a specialist in Middle European culture and languages."

"So," interrupted Evonn, "that's why you took over the questioning from Mr. Adamson."

"Exactly. You were filmed, fingerprinted, and questioned so swiftly, Evonn, you may not have realized all that went on. Do you remember when I asked you about the geography of the Bihor mountain area where you grew up?"

Evonn knitted his brows, "Sort of."

"Well, at that point I switched languages on you. You never even noticed the change from English into your native dialect."

Evonn looked chagrined. "I guess by now I'm at home in either language. Anyway, I was so nervous I couldn't think straight."

. "That's just what Adamson wanted. We knew then that you were genuinely connected in some way with the political refugee, Grigory Metvedenko. But your demand for a personal interview with him is not only puzzling, it poses security risks that can't possibly be put aside until we understand your motives. There is, you see, one major flaw in the information you have given us."

"What is it?" Both boys spoke at once.

"Metvedenko was never married and had no children."

The two boys looked at each other for a moment. Then Stefan said, "If we really open up to you, Mr. Griggs, will you help us find Dr. Metvedenko?"

"I give you my word that I will help you look for him."

"Look, Mr. Griggs, there's no sense wasting time on details you'll have to check out later anyway. I'll just tell you this. Thirteen years ago when Metvedenko defected to the United States, he left a powerful enemy behind—a certain Dr. Igor Zorak. After Metvedenko's plane accident, Zorak took some skin cells from the severed little finger of Metvedenko's right hand. We're not simply Dr. Metvedenko's sons, we're his clones!"

Griggs's right hand convulsed into a fist and smashed down with such force that the ring on his little finger gouged an ugly gash in the wooden tabletop.

Evonn's eyes flew open at the sound. When he saw the man's face, he nodded solemnly.

"It's true, Mr. Griggs. This guy Zorak is inhuman. Our friends in Stovlatz helped us get away from him, but he sent Peter Rubjak and some others after us. That's why we went into hiding and tried to change our appearances. We know him; Zorak will never give up!"

An insistent bleeping noise broke in on their conversation. Mr. Griggs flipped open his intrahospital telecom. "Mr. Griggs," said an officious voice, "there is a call on a private line from a Mr. Adamson. Please take it in the security office."

With a dazed expression still on his face, Mr. Griggs rose and left the room.

"How about that?" remarked Evonn cheerfully. "That guy believes us. I just wish the doctor would hurry up and release me, I feel much better."

Just as he was about to sink his teeth into the sweet oozy center of a tart, a knock sounded at the door. It was the driver who had taken them to the hospital.

"Hello, boys," he said pleasantly. "Mr. Adamson sends word that he's spoken to the doctor and since the sonogram showed only superficial cuts, you can leave. Tomorrow at one o'clock, Evonn, you have an appointment for a checkup. Mr. Griggs is still involved on the communicator, but he'll see you here again tomorrow." With a wave of his hand he was gone.

Evonn looked at his brother with a smile. "Do you get the feeling that we're being sent home?"

Stefan was staring at his timepiece. "That's fine. We have to go anyway. I just remembered—Rosa's birthday party!"

"Wow!" Evonn slid off the bed. "I'll get my shoes on while you write a note for Griggs."

Stefan pulled a pencil out of his pocket and spread out one of the white table napkins.

Dear Mr. Griggs,
    Sorry to leave in such a hurry. Thanks for everything. See you here tomorrow at 1:00.
                    Your friends,
                    Stefan and Evonn

P.S. We'll pick up Donner on the way out.

"Hurry up!" called Evonn from the hallway. "We're already late for the party!"

14

STEFAN, Evonn, and Donner burst in on a sober birthday feast. Abuela had set a lighted cake in front of Rosa, who sat alone at the table. Immediately all was pandemonium. Rosa tried to hug both boys at once and exclaimed over Donner, who stood waving his tail. "See, Abuela," she shouted, "I told you the boys would get back in time!"

Abuela took Evonn's bandaged head between her thin hands and rocked it back and forth wordlessly.

"Tell us what happened," cried the girl breathlessly.

The boys collapsed onto the nearest seats and told an abbreviated version of what had taken place that afternoon.

After a short silence, Rosa turned her attention to the dog. "Is he a present for me?" she asked. "Did you bring him for my birthday?"

Stefan looked stricken with guilt, but Evonn picked up Rosa's cue and quickly agreed. "You guessed it, Rosa. His name is Donner." Evonn's voice grew stronger as a new thought occurred to him. "He's a guard dog, Abuela. You can take him along on your taco route and he'll be a wonderful protector for Rosa and you when we're gone."

Abuela stroked Donner with a knowledgeable hand. "This German shepherd is a thoroughbred," she said. "What about his owner?"

"He's being sent to a new location and can't keep him," replied Stefan. "Donner really needs a new home."

"Well, we'll see how it works out."

Rosa was delighted. She knelt on the floor beside the big dog. Donner sniffed her delicately and then offered her his paw.

"Oh, what a smart dog," breathed the girl. "What a wonderful birthday present!"

The flickering birthday candles and the happy faces gathered around the table suddenly blurred before Stefan's eyes.

"What a wonderful ending to an absolutely awful day," said Evonn, echoing his brother's thoughts.

The next morning Rosa and Abuela left quietly without arousing the exhausted boys. They took Donner with them.

Later over a sparse breakfast, Evonn remarked happily, "Abuela isn't wasting any time trying him out as a watchdog. Wasn't my idea a stroke of genius?"

Stefan smiled. "Yes it was, O Modest One. We'll have to tell Griggs what we did with Donner. But should we tell him about living down here?"

"I don't know." Evonn shattered a brittle taco in one hungry bite. "Mr. Griggs seems like a great guy, but sometimes he gets an awfully weird expression on his face when he looks at us."

"Well, he never met up with clones before," exclaimed Stefan bitterly. "I thought we'd decided not to tell anyone about that except Metvedenko himself . . . and here we are, spreading it all over the place."

"We had to tell him. If Peter found us, so can Zorak's other apes. Griggs may be our best contact now," Evonn replied.

"At least he knows we need help. He almost got a taste of Peter Rubjak's knife himself yesterday." Stefan shook his head, frowning. "I just can't understand why Peter drew a knife on you, Evonn. If he meant to harm us, he would have used his gun. But that wouldn't make sense either since Dr. Zorak wants us back alive. Didn't Peter say anything at the time?"

"Yeah, he called me a thief . . . and he started pulling at the jacket I was wearing. Can you believe it? His dumb leather jacket. Then he said something about 'the money' being right at his fingertips."

"Was that when he drew out the knife?" gasped Stefan. "Evonn, do you think it's possible that the money you found could have . . .?"

The boys raced over to Evonn's bedroll. They spread Peter's jacket on the concrete floor and ripped open the lining. A few minutes later two stunned boys sat back on their heels staring at small piles of neatly bound bills. A worn envelope lay beside them.

"You must have dropped that first five hundred-dollar bill yourself, Evonn—the one we found in the men's room."

"Yeah. Now I remember hearing something rip when I yanked the belt tighter. Let's see what's inside that envelope."

Stefan unfolded four sheets of paper and held them up to the lamplight. "This is a letter written to Peter on stationery from the Stovlatz Research Station, and it's signed 'Z'!"

Evonn scanned the next sheets rapidly. "And here's one in that same code I saw back at the hotel," he cried. "See this— CL–1, and here's CL–2 down at the bottom. These papers definitely link Zorak with Peter Rubjak."

Stefan dropped the four pages and wiped his fingers on his pants. "I don't want anything to do with this stuff, even the money. It's contaminated."

Evonn rolled the money and the papers together in the leather jacket. "We'll decide about that later. Right now we'd better stash it somewhere. Griggs will think we ran out on him if we don't show up at the hospital."

The boys wedged the jacket out of sight between the uppermost steam pipes.

In the midst of pulling on a heavy sweater, Evonn paused. "I don't have a cap. I left it in the subway yesterday."

"Okay, go directly to the hospital by way of the steam

tunnel entrance," called Stefan. "I'll stop and buy a new sportscap."

When Stefan arrived at the hospital, he found Mr. Griggs and Evonn waiting for him in the outer office. Evonn now had only a small compress on his temple.

As Evonn adjusted his new cap, Mr. Griggs fixed the boys with a cold look. "Why did you two disappear on me so suddenly last night?" he asked. "By the time I got Adamson off the line, you had gone."

"We were *told* to go," exclaimed Stefan. "While you were gone, the CIA man who drove us here came in and said that Mr. Adamson wanted us to go home. We were told to meet you here today when Evonn had his bandage changed."

Mr. Griggs's face darkened with anger. "Mr. Adamson and I have had some differences of opinion lately." Abruptly he changed the subject. "Let's have lunch. I've made arrangements for us to eat in the doctor's cafeteria downstairs."

The cafeteria was bustling with doctors, some still in their work smocks. Stefan and Evonn sat happily before similar plates of roast beef and mashed potatoes with spinach.

Mr. Griggs watched them with a smile on his face. "That's one of my favorite meals, too," he said. Then, settling back in his chair, he remarked, "You two gypsies don't seem to be suffering much remorse for that vicious mugging you committed yesterday in the abandoned subway."

Evonn immediately choked on a wad of mashed potatoes and Stefan's fork froze midway to his mouth. "Mugging?" he gasped. "What are you talking about?"

Griggs laughed aloud, evidently enjoying their reactions. "Mr. Adamson let me read Peter Rubjak's statement this morning. Peter claims that he was innocently walking his pet dog when he heard moans of pain coming from inside an unused subway station. He rushed down to help, but the cries led him ever farther inside. Then, suddenly, two boys jumped out of the darkness and demanded his money. No sooner had Peter wrestled a knife away from one boy than an older man appeared to join the attack. Peter threw the knife at him but was soon overpowered and left to die."

"B-but you were there," cried Stefan, stammering in distress. "Surely you don't believe his story!"

"No, of course I don't," the man assured him. "But there were some at the CIA who thought it worth investigating.

You both seem to be acquainted with Peter. Adamson is curious about your connections with such a notorious double-agent. We recognized him by his tendency to work with a highly trained dog, and we discovered he had been rushing the training of a new one, a German shepherd."

"Peter is a double-agent?" cried Stefan. "How could he have fooled Janos and the others so completely?"

"What *others*, Stefan?" interrupted Griggs. "If you hope to be trusted, you must trust me now. Go back to the beginning of your story and tell me all the details."

"Okay. We've told you so much already, we may as well tell you the rest," Evonn said with resignation.

It took some time for the boys to fill Griggs in on their earlier adventures. When they finished, Griggs sipped his coffee slowly for a minute. Then he said, "Rubjak was a perfect choice for Dr. Zorak. He could easily infiltrate a band of amateurs such as you described."

"Stefan and I were sure that Peter was a crook!" exclaimed Evonn triumphantly. "Did the CIA get him to tell where Zorak is now?"

"Oh, no," answered Griggs. "Peter hasn't confessed to a thing. He insists that he never saw you before or heard of a Dr. Zorak. Tell me, boys, have you two been staying with the old lady in those tunnels ever since Peter first tried to turn you over to Zorak?"

"How did you know about her?" demanded Stefan.

"Adamson had you followed when you left the hospital last night," Griggs replied. "Don't be angry, he did it partly for your sake. He's posted some undercover agents down there for your protection."

"Evonn and I had hoped to keep those people out of our affairs, Mr. Griggs. We'd hate to repay their kindness by bringing the authorities down on their heads."

Griggs pushed back his chair. "They'll be left alone for the time being," he said.

Evonn turned to Stefan and an understanding passed between them. "We're sure that Abuela will soon have enough money to move out anyway."

"Now that you know all about us, do you think Mr. Adamson will let us see Dr. Metvedenko?" asked Stefan. "He is the only one who can decide how to help us."

"When I tell him what I found out this morning, I am certain that he will arrange a meeting soon." Mr. Griggs put on his overcoat.

"What shall we do now. Mr. Griggs?" said Evonn.

"Go back to your friends. Tell them only that you may be leaving soon. A messenger whom you know will contact you soon. And be more careful than you've ever been before!" He rose and laid a hand briefly on each of their heads. Then he hurried away.

A few minutes later when the boys returned to the tunnels, Evonn paused at the entrance to their own branch and looked about.

"If some undercover agent is down here guarding us, he must be rolled up inside one of these steam pipes!" he said with a chuckle.

The next evening, at almost that same spot, a familiar figure stopped the boys. It was the CIA chauffeur who had driven them to the hospital. He brought the long-awaited message. "Tomorrow!" he said. "You two are to go to the parking lot behind the precinct station at One hundred seventy-ninth Street at one o'clock. You will be driven across the river and northward to Cliffside Manor Estates, where the meeting will be held."

Without another word, the man turned and slipped quietly into the gloom.

The boys looked at each other with mounting excitement. The meeting with Metvedenko at last! They had belongings to pack, arrangements to make, and errands to run. All must be ready before noon the next day.

CHAPTER

15

EVONN set two water bags carefully on the floor beside the brass standpipe. Holding the key to the polished metal door behind it, he scanned the corridor of the office building. No one was in sight except—was that Stefan?

"Why are you up here, Stefan?" Evonn asked in surprise as his brother's figure drew near. "We shouldn't be together, especially today."

"We just got an emergency message from Adamson." Stefan seemed upset. "Something has come up and he needs to talk to us right away. He's waiting at an apartment about two blocks away from here."

"Adamson? That's really strange. I hope this doesn't mean that the meeting with Metvedenko will be delayed," Evonn groaned. "Here, grab one of these water bags. Abuela needs them, and maybe we should get our clothes and stuff."

"No! I mean, we'll have to do that later. We've got to go right away." He brushed nervously at a lock of chestnut hair that hung over his forehead. "You follow me. Be sure to keep me in sight."

Evonn shoved the bags behind the standpipe. "Okay, Stefan. Hey, I thought you were going to wash out that dye before we meet Metvedenko."

"Oh, I was . . . I started to, but then this happened." He strode quickly away from Evonn.

The two boys made their way swiftly through the usual crowd of shoppers strolling the avenue beneath the plaza dome. Once outside the enclosed area, the cold took Evonn's breath away.

As they cut across the park, Evonn heard a shout and Rosa appeared, running over the grass with Donner loping at her side.

"Hi, Evonn," she said, drawing up next to him, "where are you two going in such a hurry?"

Evonn paused and whistled shrilly to Stefan, who slowed down but continued walking. What a time to answer questions, and Rosa always wanted to know more than she should be told.

"Stefan and I have a load of errands to run today," he answered.

Rosa was not to be put off so easily. "Abuela is going to have one of her famous battles with the housing authorities this afternoon, so we came home early. Tell me what you're doing, Evonn. Maybe I can think of a way to help."

Evonn saw Stefan gesture angrily and then walk back. Donner growled as he grabbed Evonn's arm and pulled him abruptly away.

"Come back here, Stefan," Rosa called, "I want to ask you something."

"Don't bother me now!" He shouted the words over his shoulder without looking at the girl.

Evonn glanced apologetically at Rosa as he hurried off. She was staring after them, her face white with hurt.

"I can't believe you, Stefan," she yelled. "See if I ever bother *you* again!"

It wasn't like Stefan to cut Rosa off like that, thought Evonn, breaking into a run. Stefan must really be worried about this change in plans. He rounded the corner just in time to see his brother mount the steps of an old brownstone house and disappear inside. When Evonn reached the door, he found it open. Entering quickly, his eyes searched the foyer, but there was no sign of Stefan. A steep staircase hugged the wall to the left and wound upward for three flights. At the top he glimpsed Stefan's head at the bannister railing.

"Up here," came the whispered call.

But when Evonn reached the third floor, no one was in sight. This top landing was larger than the others. It was sparsely furnished with an antique mirrored hat rack in which the weak winter sun was reflected from a skylight overhead. To Evonn's relief, Stefan now appeared at an apartment door and beckoned to him.

The moment Evonn stepped inside, the paneled door swung shut behind him. A thick arm wrapped around his neck, jerking him backward. His right sleeve was shoved upward, and Evonn felt something sharp pierce the flesh of his forearm.

"Stefan!" he screamed, struggling to free himself. Then his eyes came to rest on two figures standing together, watching him.

The taller of the two stepped forward into the light, a tight smile creasing the skin on his narrow, bearded face. "Wel-

come CL–2," he purred. "You don't know how happy I am to have you with me again."

Dr. Zorak! A jolt of terror shot through Evonn as he recognized the face that had haunted him ever since he and Stefan had escaped from Stovlatz months before. He lunged to one side.

The boy beside Zorak made a gesture of protest as Evonn's captor tightened his grip from behind.

"Help me, Stef–!" Evonn's cry was choked off abruptly when the iron arm holding him drove upward against his jaw.

"The rope, Niko!" snapped Dr. Zorak.

Niko? Evonn watched, amazed, as the other boy approached him with a coil of nylon cord. 'They've drugged me,' he thought dully.

Evonn felt himself being bound and lifted onto a couch. The room began to spin, to elongate and recede from his view as if he were looking through the wrong end of a telescope. Concentrating fiercely, he brought it back into focus again.

The harsh voice of Dr. Zorak sounded nearby. "Hurry, Niko, get that dye washed out of your hair. You're wasting valuable time."

Again it was the boy who responded to Dr. Zorak's command. His figure blurred as he moved into an adjoining room. Blinking frantically to clear his vision, Evonn found the eerily enlarged head of Dr. Zorak staring down at him.

"Now, Evonn," he said, "it is time for you to answer some questions. My men who infiltrated your steam tunnels have been very clever, but there are a few details that must be confirmed."

"NO! . . . No! . . . no!" The hollow voice was Evonn's own, its echo reverberating into eternity.

Dr. Zorak chuckled dryly. "Oh yes, you will answer me.

You are no longer capable of resistance. I must have the truth. We already know that a meeting has been arranged between you two clones and Grigory Metvedenko. My first question is this—has the exact time of that meeting been established?"

Evonn shut his eyes and emptied his mind of everything save that one word—'NO'.

Dr. Zorak repeated the question.

Carefully, Evonn stretched his lips, his tongue toward that brief 'no'. But his trembling mouth said 'Yes'. And 'yes' again, and on it went until his mind was drained of all it knew of time and place, of when and where and who. By the end of Zorak's questioning, tears of frustration soaked the cushion on either side of Evonn's head.

From the foggy edges of his field of vision, the other boy spoke unexpectedly, "Stop it, Dr. Zorak!" he cried. "He's told it all. Can't you leave him alone now?"

"Very well. But do you see how easily this can be accomplished with the proper drugs? Do you realize what could happen if that turncoat Metvedenko got his hands on these boys? All the scientific secrets of Stovlatz would fall into enemy hands!"

Evonn's cry of protest died in his throat, for the boy stepped closer and now Evonn could see that he was dressed in clothes exactly like his own! The sweater and dark slacks were identical, and on the boy's head was a sportscap like the one that had become Evonn's own special trademark!

His brain felt numbed; and although Evonn still heard, only some words penetrated his understanding.

"The meeting will take place this afternoon, Niko, as we surmised," buzzed Dr. Zorak. "Listen carefully to their plan and follow along on the map. You are to meet Stefan at this point in a parking lot and be driven upriver to a cliffside manor that is well within the expected range. Remember, the less you say, the fewer possibilities of mistakes—and keep that collar buttoned high above your scar."

"Are you sure that your strategy will work, Dr. Zorak," asked the boy, "and that no one will be hurt?"

"Only if you play your part well," Zorak replied severely. "Your job is to deactivate their communications center. At the proper time, you must activate the directional button that will also release the gas pellet concealed in your cap. Its range is limited, so place it on target. We in the minicopters will lob enough cannisters of nerve gas to saturate the entire area. When you wake up again, Niko, we will all be airborne together and on our way home. You will be a hero!"

"But what if . . ."

"Nikolai Yuristovich!" interrupted Dr. Zorak sharply. "A soldier must follow orders. If you do not, I cannot guarantee the safety of this misguided youth, of Stefan—or of *anyone else!*"

The voices faded as they moved away from Evonn. A door slammed and footsteps came back into the room. Zorak bent over him again, his cold fingers probing for Evonn's neck pulse.

"Well, well, Evonn. You are fading fast. Not so fast, I hope, that you failed to recognize the third clone-brother, Nikolai. A-ha, I can see by your eyes that you do understand me. Good fellow, Niko—perhaps a bit more easily led than Stefan or you. The results of a strict military upbringing, no doubt. How little you three matter to me now that I have my chance to secure the biggest prize of all—Grigory Metvedenko!"

A low moan escaped Evonn's nerveless lips.

Dr. Zorak's long teeth showed briefly in a soundless laugh. "Amazing, my boy, you are still with me. Then you shall know that in this deadly game Niko is my wild card. He has already impersonated Stefan, and now he is impersonating you. Niko is the surprise element that your clever CIA couldn't possibly anticipate. As for you, Evonn, you are the ace up my sleeve. First my informant, and now my hostage—just to assure my win!"

Zorak's face descended so close to Evonn's that his coarse beard prickled the boy's cheek. "As you sleep, Evonn, dream of this: Metvedenko shall be destroyed by his own cells, in the persons of Stefan, Evonn, and Niko!"

CHAPTER

16

STEFAN'S timepiece had registered eleven o'clock when he said good-bye to Abuela and left the tunnels. This was the day that he and Evonn had awaited so long, and now he only wished that it were over, that he already knew what plans Metvedenko had in mind for the future of his two clone-sons.

Entering the parking lot behind the police precinct station, Stefan saw that Mr. Griggs was already there, pacing nervously between the rows of cars. As he approached, Stefan realized that his friend had never seen him before without the chestnut dye in his hair.

"This is the real me, Mr. Griggs," he said. "Do you recognize me?"

Griggs put an arm around Stefan's shoulder and gave him a squeeze. "I surely do, Stefan. In fact, now I recognize you more than ever. Where is your CIA bodyguard? Did you have any trouble on the way?"

"I didn't see anything unusual. Abuela warned me that there is another big fight going on in the tunnels among those druggies, so I took the shortcut."

"What about Evonn?" asked the man, instantly alert.

"He had an errand to run. We didn't plan to come here together, of course, but don't worry about Evonn; he knows the tunnels better than I do."

Griggs summoned a dark-suited young man and reported what Stefan had told him.

"I wasn't sure that we'd see you until we got to the manor house. Are you going to drive up there with us?" asked Stefan.

"I insisted on it." Griggs flushed. "Adamson's latest decisions have come as a bit of a surprise to me. I just hope you and Evonn won't be caught in some kind of cross fire."

Stefan was about to question that cryptic remark when a boy in a sportscap dashed into the compound. "Why are you running, Evonn?" Stefan called out.

"I think someone was following me," the boy answered, pulling his sportscap securely into place.

Stefan laughed. "I felt that way, too. Maybe our CIA bodyguards finally showed up," he said. "Anyway, you don't need to bother with that sportscap anymore. From now on, we can be ourselves."

Stefan reached out to grab the cap, but with a sharp, chopping blow, his brother deflected the outstretched hand. "Oh, no you don't, Stefan," he said. "I've become too fond of this cap to give it up now!"

Griggs joined them. "Take it easy, you two. I guess we're all a little jumpy. That's our car over there; it should be ready now."

They walked over to a low green sedan. Mechanics with earphones and various electronic gadgets were reassembling one of its rear panels.

"What are they doing to the car?" asked Stefan.

"Checking it over," Griggs answered. He approached the head mechanic. "Are you finished? We have to leave in one minute."

"Oh, you people can climb in now if you want. The driver will be here directly," the mechanic replied. "We've turned this thing inside out, Mr. Griggs, and I can assure you that there's not a bugging device within a mile."

Stefan thought Mr. Griggs looked annoyed that the fellow had said so much in front of them. He climbed into the back seat beside Evonn. Mr. Griggs took the single seat, facing the boys.

No sooner were they settled than a young man in a sports

jacket jumped into the driver's seat, and with a roar of the motor, they took off.

As they drove through the city streets, Stefan craned his neck, observing their progress with interest. He rapped his knuckles on the window beside him and smiled wryly across at Mr. Griggs. "Bulletproof glass—escort car following half a block behind us—driver who radios in to checkpoints as we pass—nothing at all unusual about this outing!"

They crossed the bridge without speaking further. Below them the river's edge was crocodile-toothed with jagged ice. Soon they were traveling on a dual parkway through a wooded area, and here and there Stefan could see the river gleaming in the distance, where it flowed beneath the granite cliffs of the Palisades.

Stefan was too excited to remain quiet for long. He looked over at Mr. Griggs, sitting tensely across from him wrapped in thought. Even Evonn seemed to have sunken into a reverie. Stefan concentrated for a few moments, looking at his brother, but was unable to break into his thoughts. Involuntarily, his head turned to the solemn man across from him.

"Why are you so worried, Mr. Griggs? Don't you think Metvedenko will show up?"

Griggs seemed startled. "Well, I am concerned about some details, Stefan, but not about Metvedenko. He'll be there."

"How can you be so sure? Have you seen him, Mr. Griggs?" asked Stefan.

"To tell you the truth, I have. Very recently." Griggs's face relaxed into a smile.

"What? You've seen Metvedenko? Why didn't you tell us? Does he know . . . all about us?" Stefan's eager outburst faltered and he asked soberly, "Mr. Griggs, will he be able to accept us? I mean, he's perfectly normal; we're the ones who are clones. Do you think he could ever consider himself—our father?"

Out of the corner of his eye, Stefan saw Evonn's head snap up as if he had been suddenly struck.

Mr. Griggs leaned forward and said earnestly, "Boys, I'm certain that Metvedenko thinks of you as his sons. But, Stefan, you are not 'only' a clone! You are a brother—and a friend."

A glowing smile spread across Stefan's face. "Maybe now I can be a son, too. Doesn't that sound great, Evonn?"

He turned and found Evonn huddled into the corner of the seat. His face had a pale, bewildered look that shocked Stefan.

"What's wrong, Evonn? Don't you feel well?" he asked.

Griggs placed a questioning hand on the boy's arm, but it was quickly shaken off. "I don't know what's happening around here," he muttered, his face to the window. "All this talking and riding is getting on my nerves. Are we almost there?"

The driver looked back over his shoulder and answered the question. "We should arrive in a few minutes," he said. "Take a good look at the architecture of this place as we approach. It's really unusual. The manor house has four levels, and it was built right into the rock walls of the Palisades."

"It must have a wonderful view," said Stefan. "Is that why it was chosen for this particular meeting?"

"Bright boy," said the driver. "The manor house is near the city, yet it's on high ground so we have an excellent overview of all the air, land, and water approaches. Not even a lizard could sneak onto the property without being spotted by one of our devices."

The road zigzagged downward across the face of the stockadelike cliffs. Gradually the trees began to thin out and soon the manor house itself came into sight. The arrival of the automobile signaled a bustle of activity at the house. Four

dark-suited agents hurried forward to escort Griggs and the boys inside.

"I have some business to attend to now, but I'll see you soon," said Mr. Griggs with an encouraging smile.

The boys were shown into a large room enclosed on three sides by floor-to-ceiling glass walls. Somehow this long-awaited introduction to their clone-father wasn't working out the way Stefan had pictured it. The whole atmosphere of this place was aloof and businesslike. It made Stefan feel totally unimportant. Once again he tried to communicate his uneasiness to Evonn but found that his brother's attention was absorbed elsewhere. Evonn had entered a small alcove off the main room where a military-type communications post had been set up. A tanned young woman sat before a console of radar screens and video scanners. As the boys watched, she leaned over a speaker built into the desk, and the boys could hear her warning off-post operatives.

"Two more minutes to zero hour," she said briskly. "Remain in 'hold' position until either a red-alert or an all-clear signal is received. I repeat . . ."

Stefan walked over to Evonn and whispered, "What do you make of all this?"

"Routine precautions," he replied, shrugging his shoulders. "Metvedenko should be here any minute." He took off his sportscap and smoothed his thick black hair. Seeming unsure of what to do with the cap, he fiddled with the top button for a moment and tossed it carelessly on the command-post desk.

Stefan could feel a growing air of anticipation in the big house now. To hide his own excitement, he busied himself with a pair of binoculars that had lain on the window ledge.

"Wow!" he said, interested in spite of himself, "these binoculars are fantastic. I can see every feather on that bird way out over the river!"

"Let me see!" Evonn's voice said in his ear, and the glasses were abruptly snatched out of Stefan's hands.

Stefan's growl of protest was stilled as several men entered through a door at the rear of the room. At the same moment, the air outside the huge windows began to pulsate with the throb of motors. Stefan swung his head around in astonishment and saw three incredibly compact minicopters descend like spiders on invisible threads and bear directly toward the glass-fronted manor house.

At Stefan's side, Evonn seemed frozen in place, the binoculars trained on the oncoming minicopters. Then he shouted frantically. "*No!* You're making a mistake; those are M-300 Laser-destroyers! Dr. Zorak, what are you doing?"

As he shouted, the closest minicopter made a wide pass in front of the manor house. Inside the machine, Stefan could see a gunner swing up his weapon, and instantly a row of tiny evergreens on the terrace toppled and fell along a pencil line of smoking destruction.

Glassy-eyed with astonishment, Stefan watched his brother suddenly drop the binoculars and race across the room to the command post. He snatched his sportscap from the desk and depressed the button on the top. Then, leaning across the already-unconscious agent, he activated the red-alert signal. The distance speaker was only inches from his face, and as he turned, he shouted into it, "Stop, Zorak! You'll kill us all!"

Stefan's first thought was that Evonn had suddenly gone mad. But now, seeing him nimbly dodge past three oncoming men and speed purposefully to the rear of the manor house, he was filled with a dull, sick rage. Leaping after the retreating figure, Stefan screamed, "Evonn! Don't run away, you've got to explain!"

But Evonn kept running.

CHAPTER
17

OUTSIDE the window of the manor house, the roar of weaponry was followed by a deafening explosion. Stefan turned to see a minicopter burst into flame. The huge tinted window shimmied like a wall of gelatin and then shattered, throwing sheets of glass into the room. Shock waves of cold air sent Stefan reeling down the corridor.

The boy ahead of him never paused. He dashed along the corridor faster than Evonn had ever run. Stefan saw him dart through the now-unguarded door. Once out in the open, he headed for the iron gate that led to the driveway. Frantically he struggled to free the latch.

A second's advantage was all that Stefan needed. Throwing himself forward in a desperate lunge, Stefan closed his fingers about the other boy's shirt collar, and, with a tearing wrench, he dragged him to the ground. Inexplicably, Stefan felt the body beneath him go slack.

Stefan straddled the boy and turned him over. For a long minute two pairs of gold-flecked amber eyes met. Then Stefan's stunned gaze followed the line of the boy's chin and exposed neck to a livid scar that lay revealed by his torn shirt collar. It snaked downward as far as Stefan could see.

"You're not Evonn!" he gasped. "Who are you?"

"My name is Niko, and I am the third clone-brother!" said the boy urgently. "Listen to me, Stefan, you must believe that I'm telling the truth. I was tricked by Zorak. Evonn is his prisoner right now and we must get to him before Zorak does!"

Stefan trembled. He couldn't gamble with Evonn's life! He

had to follow his instincts and trust this boy who was so obviously his clone.

"All right," Stefan said hoarsely, "we'll go together. But I'm warning you that if you try to slip away, or if anything happens to Evonn . . ."

"I know," said Niko, rising. Immediately he became briskly practical. "Zorak was in one of those minicopters. It veered away at the first sign of trouble. He'll have some plan to get back across the river without detection. But we must do it faster. Let's get a car!"

Stefan took one look back at the flaming manor house and gave up any thought of help. He raced after Niko to the driveway, where five vehicles were parked. Niko jumped into the driver's seat of a military staff car and slipped his hand down along the inner door.

"A-ha, military people are the same all over the world." Triumphantly, he waved a set of keys. "Can you drive?"

Stefan shook his head.

"I drove a tank one summer," Niko said confidently. After some loud clanking and grinding, the motor jerked into life. "It works, let's get . . ." His voice broke as a gun was leveled at him through the open car window.

"Don't move!" said Mr. Griggs. His soot-smudged face was grooved with sorrow. "How could I have been so wrong about you boys? I must take you back to the authorities."

"Mr. Griggs, please listen," begged Stefan. "I didn't know this until now, but this isn't Evonn! He is a third clone—show him the scar, Niko. Evonn has been captured by Zorak. Niko was tricked into helping him."

"It's true, sir," added Niko. "I know how bad all this must sound to you, but remember it was I who activated the 'red-alert' signal when I saw what Zorak was up to. Only one thing matters now, and that is to get to Evonn before it's too late."

Mr. Griggs's face hardened. "I can't take any more chances with you two," he said. "I'll check out your story, but you must stay here under guard." He whipped out his portable communicator and spoke into it urgently. The tiny amplifier released an outburst of simultaneous transmissions. Many voices overrode one another, all shouting commands.

"You'll never get through on that thing, Mr. Griggs. Please come with us," Stefan begged again. "If Niko isn't telling the truth, I don't care what you do with us."

After a short pause, Griggs nodded and jumped into the back of the car, his gun drawn.

Niko shifted into first gear and the staff car careened down the drive and onto the zigzag road.

"I have to ask you this, Niko," said Stefan, clinging to the seatback, "why did you help Zorak in the first place, and what turned you against him at the last minute?"

Niko answered in brief, compact sentences. "First Zorak told me I was a clone, but not who my father was. Then he said that my two clone-brothers had been brainwashed by a defector named Metvedenko. He told me you were in America and would soon be shipped to an interrogation center."

Stefan was only vaguely aware that the automobile had swerved onto the grass median and was now passing a long line of traffic. "What a pack of lies!" he cried angrily, "but what were you supposed to do?"

"Zorak said I could help save you. The plan was to snatch you away at the last minute. Zorak wanted you two back at Stovlatz—and he wanted Metvedenko to face charges as a traitor."

"But, Niko, what made you change your mind about Zorak's intentions?" Stefan asked, waiting impatiently as Niko slammed on the brakes, narrowly missing a cargo trailer.

"Stop the car!" called Mr. Griggs weakly from the back seat.

"Why didn't you tell me you don't know how to drive this thing?"

"Well, you couldn't hold a gun on us and operate a car at the same time," answered Stefan innocently. "Besides, I thought Niko was doing fine considering he's only driven a tank before."

Griggs groaned, and as soon as the car stopped he crawled into the front seat with the boys. Stefan noticed that his gun was tucked away into a shoulder holster. He pulled out into traffic. "Tell the rest of your story later, Niko. I've heard enough."

The short winter afternoon was beginning to wane when the staff car pulled in front of the brownstone apartment house.

"What do I hear?" Griggs asked as the boys piled out of the car. His head was back, his eyes searching the roofline.

Stefan heard a familiar throbbing sound somewhere above them. "The minicopter!"

"Stay behind me!" ordered Mr. Griggs. His laser pistol freed the front door locks and the three sped silently up the winding staircase. They approached the upper landing cautiously. The throbbing noise was louder here.

"Rooftop," whispered Niko.

"Stay clear of it, the pilot will be armed," warned Griggs. "Zorak is probably inside the apartment right now with Evonn. We'll have to break in this door without warning him. Then you two get out of here. All together—*NOW!*"

The molded wood splintered under their combined weight. Mr. Griggs leaped into the room with his gun raised. The two boys fanned out on either side of him.

"Well, well, look who's here," snarled the voice of Dr. Zorak. "The CIA and my own two wonder boys!"

Stefan's heart stopped beating when he saw that Zorak was holding a limp figure propped up before him.

"Move away from that boy, Zorak!" commanded Mr. Griggs in a hoarse voice.

"No, Evonn will accompany me every step of the way out of this room," drawled Zorak. "As you see, he is not feeling quite himself at the moment. I doubt that you will try to shoot me while I'm holding him in front of me. Just to make sure, I shall have to ask you to drop that gun out the window."

"Not on your life!" growled Griggs.

"Drop it for Evonn's life then," purred Zorak, "because he won't live much longer if I use this needle I'm holding against his jugular vein. I assure you that the dosage is lethal." Zorak's voice became steely. "Drop it out the window!"

Reluctantly, Mr. Griggs opened the window and tossed his weapon into a courtyard below.

"Good!" said Zorak. "Now if you will excuse us, come along, Clone–Two, *walk!*"

Evonn groggily obeyed the orders of the man half-supporting him.

"Wait a minute, Dr. Zorak!" Niko called out. "Take me for your hostage. I'm the one who ruined your plans. I even alerted the whole CIA security system."

Zorak kept walking. "Some day I will even that score with you, Niko. But for now I'll keep Evonn. He's drugged and not likely to give me any trouble."

Panic-stricken, Stefan watched them retreat through the doorway onto the landing.

"Get out of here, use the fire escape," Griggs commanded the two boys in a low voice. Then he strode out onto the landing.

"Igor Mihail Zorak!" Griggs's voice boomed out like the roar of a bull elephant. "I knew you for a vengeful egomaniac many years ago—but, by God, I'll call it to you now face-to-face!"

At the sound of that voice, Zorak stopped dead in his tracks. He swiveled in place like a menacing mannikin on a revolving stand.

The sun's rays slanting through the skylight bathed Griggs in a crimson glare as he slowly, deliberately wrapped his jacket around one arm and removed his glasses.

"You!" breathed Zorak, and with a mighty heave, he shoved Evonn's limp figure headlong into his adversary.

As Griggs staggered off balance, Zorak leaped forward, his long needle raised like a dagger.

Outside the building the sharp report of gunshots broke out. Zorak swung his head up, listening. Instantly Griggs dove under his upraised arm and the two men crashed to the floor.

Stefan and Niko dodged out of the apartment and dragged Evonn back inside, narrowly escaping a burst of gunfire as the rooftop door flew open and an armed man leveled his weapon at several CIA agents now swarming up the narrow staircase.

18

"IT'S NOT FAIR, I missed it all!" cried Evonn. "I'm always the one who gets knocked out or drugged. I don't even remember being brought to this CIA compound. I suppose that guy Adamson will drop by with the others—I don't like him. Finish telling me what happened before he gets his big mouth flapping in here."

"Talk about a big mouth!" Stefan laughed. "You've hardly been quiet a moment since you regained consciousness."

"Okay, then it's your turn." Evonn settled back comfortably on the couch in the private sitting room that had been provided for them.

"Well," began Stefan, "when Zorak started to lead you away, Griggs bellowed out some insult that made Zorak attack him like a raving maniac. That's when the CIA came charging inside shooting."

Evonn looked puzzled. "But how did the CIA ever locate us?" he asked. "That—that Niko was the only one who knew where I was being held."

"You'd never guess," said Stefan, smiling broadly. "It was Rosa! Miss Curiosity herself. She was so mad at the way the other 'Stefan' had brushed her off at the park that she decided to find out for herself what you were up to. So she had Donner track you to the brownstone. When only one of us ran out again, she got worried and went to tell Abuela. Abuela knew that something terrible was happening because I'd just left her a few minutes before. I couldn't have been in two places at once—in the tunnels with her and on the streets with Evonn. So they went straight to the CIA."

Evonn chuckled. "Maybe Abuela won't scold Rosa about being nosy anymore."

"But the best part," added Stefan, "is that the CIA has agreed that Rosa and Abuela should have the money as a reward. Peter denies everything anyway. I can't wait to tell them!"

A sharp rap at the door was followed by the entrance of Mr. Adamson and Niko. Adamson strode directly across to Evonn and grasped his hand. "The last time we met, Evonn, I gave you a rather bad time of it. It was our job to protect Dr. Metvedenko, and your sudden appearance posed serious complications. That, however, is all in the past now."

Adamson stepped back to look with frank curiosity at the three almost identical faces surrounding him. "Clones!" he said. "Amazing!" Then he excused himself to use the communicator in an adjoining room.

Niko looked intently from one brother to the other. Then he straightened and took a resolute step toward Evonn.

"Sorry I tricked you, Evonn," he said bluntly, "but Dr. Zorak had convinced me . . . Oh, I was an idiot! A complete idiot!"

Evonn had to smile at Niko's artless apology. His animosity faded. "Well, Stefan tells me that you got smart real fast up at that manor house," he said, "alerting the mobile units, getting Griggs and him to the brownstone, and even offering to take my place as a hostage."

Niko dismissed that with a wave of his hand. "I was responsible for you," he said, "because I let you escape from Stovlatz in the first place."

"What the devil are you talking about?" demanded Evonn.

Niko took a deep breath. "One night last June I was on security duty at Stovlatz. One of the monitors registered movement near the Outer Barrier. Although it was dark, I could make out the silhouettes of two boys. I began groping for the alarm button, but I couldn't keep my eyes off them. When they met, they hugged each other and slapped one another on the back. They were so happy that I seemed . . . that I *was* happy, too. It was weird. Somehow *I* was sharing *their* feelings. And, on an impulse, I bypassed the alarm and signaled 'All Clear'."

Evonn whistled softly. "Whew! That was Stefan and me on the night we escaped. And to think we never knew."

"No wonder you felt responsible for us later on. Did you ever figure out why you'd done it?" asked Stefan.

"Not until Zorak told me about my clone-brothers. When he said you were in danger, I felt that I had made a terrible mistake. I just had to help get you back!"

Evonn sighed. "I can understand your side of it a lot better now," he said. "I suppose Zorak told you that we'd all be brought back together and continue with our education, right?"

"He promised me!" growled Niko. "I'd never met anyone like Dr. Zorak before. I grew up at the Military Academy. Our commandant is a fine man and my good friend, he's going to help me get into cosmonaut school."

Adamson re-entered the room and stood quietly for a moment. Then he said, "You needn't concern yourselves about Dr. Zorak anymore. In the struggle to subdue him, his hypodermic needle pierced his own skin and he died from the poison."

There was a shocked silence in the room, then Adamson continued. "Perhaps I underestimated Dr. Zorak. His three-pronged attack against us today was brilliant. First, the fights in the tunnels that trapped our CIA bodyguards, then the substitution of Niko, and finally those minicopters dropping down on us from the upper cliff—unbelievable! He came closer to success than I care to think about."

Evonn stood up, his cheeks burning. "Well, I'm glad he's dead! He was evil. He manipulated people as if they were toys and even thought he could destroy them if it suited his needs."

"You're right, of course. Perhaps it was an ironic justice that he was killed by his own poison." Adamson walked toward the door. "I must go now, but first I want to thank you all for your courage and initiative in the face of danger. With your help, our operation was essentially a success. Now Dr. Metvedenko can lead a safe and productive life in this country."

After Adamson disappeared, Stefan turned to the others. "Did you notice anything strange about Adamson's summary of today's operation? He said it was a success because Zorak was caught and now Metvedenko is safe."

Niko looked up. "What about it?"

"I see what you mean, Stefan," Evonn frowned. "We thought that the whole point of the meeting today was to get us together with our clone-father so we could make some plans for our future. That part seems to have been unimportant."

"True," agreed Niko, "but Adamson's statement does reveal the CIA's strategy throughout this whole operation. They kept hoping that you two would lure Zorak out into the open so they could capture him when he went after you. But I know that after Peter Rubjak vanished, Dr. Zorak got wind of the CIA and figured there was bigger game afoot—Metvedenko himself!"

"You're saying that Stefan and I became bait!" Evonn's voice was sharp with resentment. "Sure! Zorak figured we'd lead him to Metvedenko, and the CIA figured we'd lead them to Zorak."

Stefan suddenly looked very tired. "No wonder Griggs said he hoped we wouldn't get caught in a cross fire. We did, you know, but we managed to get in a few shots of our own. Sometimes I think Griggs was the only one who cared what happened to us."

A rhythmical knock sounded at the door. "There he is now!" cried Stefan.

He was right. Mr. Griggs walked into the room looking fit despite a purple bruise on his left cheek. He put an arm around Stefan's shoulder, tousled Evonn's hair, and shook hands warmly with Niko, who had tried to back away.

"What's going on with the Clone Clan?" he asked lightly. His eyes searched their faces. "Have you got everything figured out? What's the matter with you, Niko?"

"Oh, he's embarrassed again," explained Evonn. "Every time someone walks in, he feels that he should apologize all over again."

"Not to me, Niko," said Griggs quietly. "You've made up triplefold for any past mistakes. In fact, my boys, I'm the one who owes you an apology. Mr. Adamson did warn me ahead of time that some risks had to be taken today—none of us would be really safe until Zorak was caught—but I had no idea of just how great those risks actually were."

Evonn nudged Niko. "See, even Griggs makes mistakes, so stop feeling so guilty."

Griggs hitched up the knees of his narrow trousers and settled himself on the couch. "Tell me, Evonn. How do you know so much about what Niko thinks and feels?"

Evonn was surprised at the question. "I know because we're clones. We do have a certain amount of ESP. It doesn't always work, of course, especially if both parties aren't cooperating."

"That's what happened when I was impersonating them, sir," said Niko. "I deliberately blocked the other out of my mind."

Griggs nodded. "I see, then even with clones, ESP works best as a two-way effort between sender and receiver."

Stefan studied the man who sat beside him. "All this must be leading up to something," he said.

"It is—but first I'd like to ask a few more questions. Why

did Niko have so little trouble switching from impersonating Stefan to impersonating Evonn? Why were your disguises so minimal? Weren't you afraid Zorak's men would recognize you?"

"Gosh, Mr. Griggs, our best protection was simply to avoid being seen together," said Evonn. "Beyond that, elaborate disguises didn't seem necessary."

Niko chuckled. "You two are so ordinary-looking that any camouflage would do!"

Evonn grabbed a sofa pillow and fired it at Niko. "Like you!" he chortled. "Just—like—you!"

"Just like many of us," admitted Griggs, rising. "Some people have large noses or other distinctive features. If not, then things like caps and glasses and hairstyles can make a tremendous difference in one's appearance."

He crossed the room to a mirror hanging above the fireplace and parted his own thick mane, combing it flat.

"You, Stefan," he continued, "had to use a dye to change your hair. But often nature makes its own changes—my own dark hair has become almost white."

He turned to face the suddenly silent boys.

"Or, take tinted glasses, they can serve as a mask," he said. The removal of his revealed a smiling pair of gold-flecked amber eyes.

"But if I ever needed a really convincing item to disguise myself from, say Dr. Zorak, it would be a flashy ring on my little finger. Because he knew I had lost that finger long ago. Thanks to modern medicine, it was regenerated. So a ring such as this," he drew it off, "would serve to attract attention to the finger and to hide this scar tissue."

Hardly had he finished speaking when Stefan jumped up, waving his arms above his head. "*Ya-hoo!* I can't believe it! Hey, brothers!" He turned to them and announced dramatically, "Dr. Metvedenko has finally arrived!"

EPILOGUE

"DON'T YOU two understand what's been going on?" Stefan exclaimed to his astonished brothers, "Griggs is our father! He's Grigory Metvedenko!"

Evonn rose slowly. "B-but," he stammered, "why would you have kept that a secret for so long, Mr. Griggs?"

The man before them met each pair of amber eyes in turn. "Boys, I hated that deception. Adamson insisted that you were not to know who I was until after Zorak was caught. It was a safeguard for us all. Evonn, what would have happened if you'd known my true identity when Zorak gave you that truth drug? Do you think any of us would have reached the manor house alive?"

All three boys started talking at once.

Evonn was the first to make himself heard. "Hey, Gri— Dad!" he shouted, hands on hips. "No wonder you knew I'd fall for that language switch in Adamson's office."

"And no wonder," yelled Stefan, joining Evonn, "you were so sure about what Metvedenko thought about everything."

"And now I know why you wanted me to explain about the ESP—*you* had blocked *us* out, too!" Niko lined up with the others.

Metvedenko rolled his eyes in mock terror. "Uh-oh!" he muttered. "I'd better get away from this freaky gang as fast as I can." He made a feint for the door.

"Oh, no you don't!" cried Stefan.

Although no visible sign passed among them, the three boys lunged forward in unison. And Dr. Grigory Met-

vedenko, shouting with laughter, disappeared in a bois-
terous tangle of arms and legs.